D1058726

Time
and the
Tapestry

Time
and the
Tapestry

A William Morris Adventure

JOHN PLOTZ

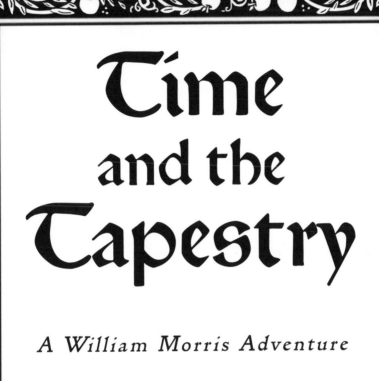

Bunker Hill Publishing

www.bunkerhillpublishing.com
Bunker Hill Publishing Inc.
285 River Road, Piermont
New Hampshire 03779, USA

10 9 8 7 6 5 4 3 2 1

Copyright text © 2014 John Plotz
Copyright illustrations © 2014 Phyllis Saroff

All rights reserved.

Library of Congress Control Number: 2013949578

ISBN 978-1-59373-145-8

Designed by JDL
Printed in China

Without limiting the rights under copyright reserved above, no part
of this publication may be reproduced, stored in or introduced into a
retrieval system, or transmitted, in any form or by any means (electronic,
mechanical, photocopying, recording or otherwise), without the prior
written permission of the publisher of this book.

The Author's royalties for this book will benefit the
William Morris Society in the United States
www.morrissociety.org

For further information on William Morris and the publisher
go to www.bunkerhillpublishing.com

For Helen Abrams (1912–2013)

Granny

CHAPTER ONE

Nobody But Us

This story begins the Friday Granny got the letter. "We regret to inform you"—she read it out to us matter-of-factly as we flopped down on our dusty old sofa— "that the age and origin of your Tapestry remain mysterious . . ."

I felt my ears go numb and I lost the rest. Ed sucked in his breath, like he'd been punched. I put my head down. I didn't want to see what Granny's face looked like, and I really didn't want her to see mine.

So we're losing the house, I told myself, *losing it, losing it, losing it.* No amount of repetition could make it sink in. It was the kind of thing that happens in old-fashioned books where kids wear flour-sack dresses and bake biscuits on a cookstove.

I started running through *if only*'s in my mind, like a filmstrip that wouldn't stop. Each picture was something that could have made it all turn out differently. *If only developers didn't want to build a mall right where our house stands. If only the museum had decided to buy up everything in our house,* or *if only Granny had sold her Arts and Crafts antiques to that rich collector with the Lexus.* Like a skipping CD, the biggest one of all kept looping back into my thoughts: *If only our parents had never gotten on that flight . . .*

Part of my brain likes to look down at life from an attic window. That part was wondering why I was letting myself get so upset over a letter. After all, Granny and Ed and I were pretty used to angry letters from the bank, or from developers who couldn't wait to get their hands on what they liked to refer to as our "developable lot."

Before the day this letter came, the Museum of Fine Arts had only meant Mr. Nazhar the curator coming over for tea and a look at some of Granny's "trrreasures." We loved the way he rolled his r's, and the soft battered briefcase that he let Ed hold on his lap during the visit. And we couldn't keep our eyes off his old-fashioned leather checkbook, which always came out toward the end.

At first he only took away beautifully printed books: "Kelmscott," Granny said reverently, even though the author's name on the crackly yellow covers might be John Keats, or John Milton, or Dante Gabriel Rossetti. Later it was ordinary things from our living room or even our kitchen—tiles, lamps, tables, glasses ("Webb glasses," said Granny once in her quietest voice, stroking them softly). Hard to believe someone would visit a museum just to see things I'd held in my hands a hundred times.

In the six years after we came to live with Granny, Mr. Nazhar came to visit a lot. He wasn't the only visitor, though. Sometimes we'd hear a roar and look out the front windows to see a bald, sweating man climbing slowly out of his shiny, sleek car: "Lexus: The Relentless Pursuit of Perfection!" Ed whispered to me once in a soft, solemn voice. Lexus guy smiled a lot, but I noticed that he always seemed to be looking right through us, as if we were a wispy curtain, barely visible, standing between him and his future Arts and Crafts collection. We never learned his name, and Granny never sold him anything. Still, I dreamed about him sometimes: I was always watching his blue Lexus driving away, sagging under the weight of whatever was crammed into it. Sometimes just chests and chairs, but once it was Granny and Ed, both rolled up in packing tape and staring back at me sadly.

Over the years it never mattered that the living room and dining room had emptied out little by little after those visits, or that overnight trips, restaurant dinners, and even movies were treats we had to plan for very carefully. No matter how bad things got, we always knew we had our insurance plan. Sell the Tapestry.

Granny always said *Tapestry* with a capital letter, like *President*. It was far and away the most beautiful thing we owned, a giant rug of gold, red, green, and mostly blue, filled with forest animals, birds, unicorns, and all manner of things that gazed down at us from a whole wall of the living room. Over the years, as one thing after another got wrapped up and carefully placed inside Mr. Nazhar's briefcase, the Tapestry started feeling bigger and bigger, like a wall map. Or, when I was feeling especially lonely, a window into another world.

The Tapestry was woven by William Morris just before he died, more than a century ago. He's Granny's favorite artist, and she's not the only one who feels that way. He's not quite teach-him-in-middle-school famous. Still, a genuine work this size, designed by him and made in his own Merton Abbey Factory by the workers that he and his daughter had trained, had to be worth way more than the little painted tiles and scraps of manuscript Mr. Nazhar had been taking lately.

So when the bank threatened to take away our house a few months ago, I barely flinched.

"The museum will help you, Granny," I announced cheerfully. "Just like before."

Mr. Nazhar loves Granny; he told her he'd trade twenty interns in black stockings for a chance to put her to work at the museum. He's always coming by to quiz her about her old days in "the Merrrton shop": I love how he always says it just exactly like that, with a kind of purr in *Merton*, and *shop* like *chop*. "And did Morris's daughter May supervise the textiles at Merrrton while you worked there, Georrrrgie?"

Granny's real name is Georgiana, which always makes me think of some Edward Gorey character in a long white gown, eating asparagus with a pearl-handled fork. She likes people to call her Georgie, or even George, but I think Georgiana suits her. Mr. Nazhar likes to eat Granny's almond macaroons and ask her long-winded questions about textiles, and woodblock printing, and a load of things that most kids only come across on a field trip to Plymouth, or a family vacation at Colonial Williamsburg.

One day, when Granny was showing him how to embroider a valence using freshly dyed indigo thread, Ed leaned over and whispered, "Jen, don't tell him that nobody cares about the stuff Granny knows anymore." I whispered back, "Nobody but *us*!" He looked down at the copper plate where I was doing my best to engrave something recognizable, using Mom's old burins and burnishers, and he gave a little nod.

The money from the museum was our lifeline. After our parents died, all of Granny's old students had stopped coming. Partly because weaving and printmaking get harder to teach with arthritis, but also because we started to scare people a bit. I think I even scared Eva sometimes, and she's supposedly my best friend. Back then, Granny was easy to classify: a lovable old immigrant (*what an adorable accent!*) with her artist daughter and a son-in-law who taught shop at the high school. It probably helped that my dad also built hardwood furniture that ended up in a lot of our neighbors' living rooms.

Things kind of changed after the accident—I mean, when it was just the three of us. Ed was only five then (I was eight) and he was liable to start yelling, really yelling for Granny's help when he couldn't get one of his notebooks exactly the way he wanted it.

Eva once told me everyone was expecting "some nice family" take us in. Granny worked hard all her life, but what she worked at never had much to do with packing lunches and showing up for school plays. Mom had been her only child, and that was forty years ago.

Still, she stuck it out, and so did we, learning her rules little by little. Whether it's fixing the lawn mower, cooking, or making new clothes, Granny will always do it first. But I better be watching so I can do it next time. And teach it to Ed the time after that: See one, do one, teach one.

On top of that, Granny somehow still manages to come up with new basketball shoes for me every season, and an endless supply of drawing paper for Ed. Even though we can't buy all the poetry books I'd like—in fact, we can't buy any—my dad left a pretty good collection, and the library is only four stops away on the subway. On a good day, maybe practicing archery in the backyard with the arrows Granny taught us to fletch, Ed will shout "Jen, Granny! We're the unholy Trinity!" and for just a minute, everything seems perfect. Almost.

Granny, meanwhile, was still reading Mr. Nazhar's letter. He really did want things to work out—said he was working on a plan that would be even better than just buying it from us, a plan that would keep us in our house and Granny connected to the museum. But the trustees of the museum, the ones with the checkbooks that really mattered, couldn't accept that the Tapestry was designed and made by William Morris and his Merton workers.

Their problem was simple: The Tapestry wasn't finished. It had

about a dozen places where the weaving just stopped, and all you could see was the bare cream-colored warp. It was like looking at a TV that was perfect in most places, but dissolved into dead pixels right where you most wanted to see.

I didn't need Mr. Nazhar to tell me about gaps in the Tapestry. Even though they'd never made me doubt the Tapestry was actu-ally by Morris, the Lost Spots (I use capital letters for them, too) haunted me. When I should have been paying attention in geogra-phy class, my brain would keep telling stories about them. About a gap in a meadow, or a clearing in the forest that looked as if some giant snaky animal had been peeled right off the picture.

Take the lower left-hand corner, where a redheaded girl in an emerald gown was stretching her arm way up beneath a blossom-ing tree. Her fingers were just about to close around a little empty circle that I could swear was meant to be an apple. Her expression had always puzzled me. It was so sad, as if she knew that her fingers were closing not on an apple, but on empty space. I was convinced that if the apple *had* been there, her expression would have changed.

Ed was more practical. He made a diagram that totaled up the number of missing square inches. "Granny," he started firmly, "I don't think there are more than a dozen gaps in this tapestry. There's this open space up here in the sky and what looks basically like a river down here, and a really fat pony, and this could be two squid quarreling over a ball of yarn, and . . ." He trailed off again, looking up at me for guidance, thinking maybe I'd tell Granny about the Lost Spots.

I couldn't do it. I slumped back on the sofa and peered over Granny's shoulder, not bothering to take off my clumsy gear bag, ignoring the way my basketball shoved into my spine. No way would the drawings I'd had Ed make, or the elaborate stories I'd tried out in front of the Tapestry, be the kind of proof Mr. Nazhar could bring to the trustees. Even he would only have smiled and looked down into his tea. His idea of evidence didn't have much to do with the stories I told. I pictured his earnest face, his mustache lightly sprinkled with almond macaroons, thinking about how it lit up when Granny produced an actual shuttle from "the Merrrton shop" or a "verrified" piece of William Morris stained glass. Why would he believe my story about a missing dragon under the oaks, or my idea of what it felt like for that girl to reach up and have her fingers close on nothing?

I could tell the letter had gotten to Granny also. All those years back in England working for the company that Morris himself had founded, all those years spent learning how to weave, to embroider, to paint tiles, and all the rest. Wasn't she, herself, all the proof Mr. Nazhar could want? *Look at these hands,* she might have said to Mr. Nazhar. *Don't you think these hands would know a Tapestry by William Morris?*

I wish," Granny began, unusually fierce, "I simply wish . . ." Ed and I shot worried glances at each other. I remembered, just once, looking inside Granny's dresser and finding a note from Aunt Cathy, Daddy's horsey sister, warning Granny how "unusual and reckless" it was for someone in her eighties to take a pair of "rambunctious children" into her house. "There are state-sponsored alternatives . . . ," the letter went on; I'd dropped it and run out of the room.

Looking at Granny now, seeing how her hand shook over the letter, I was really glad I'd never mentioned that note to Ed. "I wish," Granny said a third time, and then her face cleared and she laughed, "I wish that we could ask advice from the only truly sensible member of this family!" And she shot her usual fond look over at Mead.

Granny is very fond of fond looks, and especially fond of Mead. So am I. He's the only tame blackbird I've ever even heard of. When he's not trying to hide pebbles in my hair or peck holes in my basketball, he might be my favorite member of the family. It struck me that his cage was about the only other beautiful old thing that hadn't made its way to the museum—yet.

As usual, Mead tilted his head sideways at her and whistled softly. Then he flicked his wings a bit, and gazed up and away—remembering something, maybe. I couldn't help asking, for the millionth time, "But Granny, how do you know? You always say it was by him, but really, really, how do you know?"

Usually when I say that, she just shakes her head in that *I'm so learned, I can't help it* way. Today, though, she leaned back and polished her glasses.

"I don't think I've ever mentioned this before, Jen—" There was one of Granny's dramatic pauses, and I could hear Ed frantically flipping over pages in his notebook in case Granny said something he could add to his tidy list of Tapestry Information. "I know the Tapestry was woven by Morris," she went on finally, "because *she* told me he'd made it when she gave it to me. Along with a little poem."

As she spoke, it was like a match scratched against something in my brain and started to sputter. Ed inherited my mother's drawing ability, along with her beautiful artist's pencils. I got something else instead: these memories, so vivid but so hard to place. So, whenever I see a chubby man walking next to a slightly taller redheaded woman I get a little lump in my throat. That's obviously something about Mom and Dad, right; but what? Am I seeing some special moment, or is that image the condensed summary, like a little memory stick that I somehow loaded up with their whole lives?

This was a throat-lump memory, too, but a new one. I was in a lap, it was evening, I could see Dad in front of me with a little green book, gold lettering on the spine. I knew somehow it was an old, old poem about a girl who'd lost something. When I closed my eyes, I could even hear the rhymes.

"Queen," I whispered, and then right away: "unseen." I struggled, waiting for more to come. The lap was warm; and I was pretty sure that right next to me was a little baby sleeping (could that be Ed?).

While all those thoughts about my parents (and all my resolutions not to think about them) were running through my head, Granny smiled at me and opened her mouth to speak. Before she could, though, I suddenly said "fell and well." It felt so good, I said it again: "Fell and well!" Like picking a scab, it ached, but it felt so good. Only what did it mean?

CHAPTER TWO

Uhat's Undone

ll this time Ed had been jabber-
ing away frantically like a radio
nobody remembered to turn down. I
tuned him back in. "Jen? Granny? Can
someone please tell me what's going on?"

"It's nothing," I said quickly. "When Granny mentioned poetry
I suddenly thought about Dad reading something to me. No idea
why."

"Maybe because Dad always used to mutter poetry to himself
when he was working."

"What? That's impossible, Ed!" I said hotly. But was it? After
all, how could I remember what I'd forgotten? There were so few
memories, so many empty spaces. At least the Lost Spots in the
Tapestry had a shape, a blank to be filled in.

Granny pulled her chair past Mead's cage so that all of us faced the Tapestry. Folding Mr. Nazhar's letter and tucking it with steady hands back into its envelope, she locked her eyes on the Tapestry. "There are some memories that have been with me so long, I can hardly see them anymore. They're a part of my apprenticeship—my childhood on the wane, my youth as it gave way to age." Granny has these phrases that pour out of her and I've learned that rather than asking her to define every word, sometimes you just have to let it flow over you like a waterfall.

"What I remember about the Great Depression, in our poor little corner of London," Granny began ("Pimlico," Ed muttered, fingering the neat row of pens in his shirt pocket, "you lived in Pimlico"), "was that parents couldn't work, and children had to. I minded less than most of my friends, though, working at the Merton Abbey Factory.

"A shadow of its former self it was," Granny continued, "melting ever so slowly away since William Morris himself had died back in the 1890s. To me it was a job still, a paying job and glad to have it, thank you kindly! One day, though, when I'd just turned fifteen and gotten my first rise in pay, *she* came to sit by me at my loom. Though she was not, most definitely *not* the kind to cry at work, her eyes did seem red."

"She?" If Ed hadn't asked it, I would have.

But Granny was lost in the story already. "For a while she just sat there by me, doing the things a second pair of hands can always do at a loom—tying off the dangling weft, sliding the beater in as the heddle is raised, all those little things." While she was talking, her arms had gone into a peculiar crooked position they often fell into when she was thinking, or telling a long story, or even napping. Her left arm came straight out from her body, while her right moved in slow sweeps from her hip across her body, bouncing smoothly back when it struck, then starting its motion again.

"'I have something to give you, Georgie,' she said, 'and something to ask you.'

"I only nodded, I was that scared." ("That scared," I muttered to myself, "that scared." I try to collect all the phrases Granny uses in her England stories.)

"'It's winding up now, winding up any day,' Miss Morris said.

"I wanted to cry out that it should never end, that there was no reason Morris and Company couldn't go on weaving fabric and printing wallpaper until I had grandchildren myself.

"I only nodded, head down—I was a good girl in those days, a quiet shy girl. I couldn't stop myself, though, from blurting out, 'But I hope it's not quite over.'

"She chuckled, then grabbed my chin. It was an affectionate touch, but she made sure she could look me in the eye before she went on.

"'There's a present I want you to have before it ends,' she said flatly.

"She gave a short laugh. Looking back now I think it was a sad laugh, and maybe a bitter one. But I was only a girl. I remember thinking it was nice for May that she could laugh—but oh, how my mother was going to cry when she learned our last wages were gone.

"Miss May Morris went on, her voice sounding oddly brittle to me, vibrating a bit up and down like the pitch of the wheezy organ at church. 'You've been a good worker, Georgie; it's always a pleasure to weave with you. I can tell, I can always tell, just by watching the fingers, the ones who know where the pattern should go, who even know where the story should go . . . Do you know what I mean?'

"She gave me a sharp glance that caught me by surprise; I expect I'd just been gaping up at her like any foolish fifteen-year-old.

"'Oh yes, Miss Morris, I do,' I said nervously, before she could explain. I wish I'd let her say what she meant about how the story and the pattern go together. Even now . . ." Granny trailed off and sat staring up at the Tapestry. Ed and I shot nervous glances at each other, watching her fingers weave and unweave on top of Mr. Nazhar's letter.

"'I have a Tapestry that should stay with someone who understands it, who knows it with her hands as well as her head,'" Granny said finally: it took us a minute to realize that she was giving us May Morris's voice again.

"'You'll find it by the side door there, Friday week, properly bundled up. Bring your father to help you carry it; can you do that?'

"I nodded when she asked me that: Hadn't my father come over from Cork as a stevedore, loading and unloading ships in Liverpool and then down at the London docks as long as there was work? He could have carried three of her tapestries, I thought but didn't say.

"'There's another thing you'll carry with you,' she said, and I could hear the iron in her voice when she said it. 'Let's call it a task, or a chore, or, well, the proper word for it, Georgie, is a *geas*.'" It was a strange word: I turned it over and over on my tongue as she kept talking.

"'When you look at that Tapestry, you'll see that it's *undone*.' There was something funny in how she said that word: Did she mean that it wasn't finished? I couldn't quite say what *undone* would mean, if not that.

"'The Tapestry will be done, Georgie, it will be done in time. I can't tell you anything more than that.' I thought she was done speaking, but as I opened my mouth to agree she went on: 'But I can point the way with a poem.'"

Granny turned quickly to see if she'd surprised us. I don't know about Ed but I hadn't seen this one coming, and my face must have showed it. Satisfied, I guess, Granny gave a small smile, turned her eyes back to the Tapestry, and went on.

"There was plenty of poetry in that factory. Somebody often read to us as we worked: from *The Earthly Paradise* that William Morris himself had written, or from poems by John Keats, John Milton, Shakespeare. I even read out of some of those same little Kelmscott books Mr. Nazhar likes so much. But I'd never thought of poems as, well, guidebooks.

"Miss Morris chuckled suddenly; my skepticism must have showed. 'Well, it may be there's more to poems than you think, Georgie.'

"'I expect so, Miss Morris. At least, I hope so,' I couldn't help adding. She gave a tiny smile at that.

"'This is not a poem for writing down, Georgie. You'll learn it with me as we sit at this loom together, and it'll be written up *here*'—tapping her forehead with a straight, stiff forefinger. After a moment, she also reached over and touched my forehead with the same finger—smooth, dry, and soft."

Granny stopped speaking, though her right arm still kept up a slow, almost invisible back-and-forth.

"And did you learn it, Granny?" I asked.

"I did," Granny said. "May Morris herself sat with me the next day and taught me as we worked. In fact, the very the moment I'd finished reciting it, I had the strangest dream . . ." Her voice trailed away slowly.

"A dream, Granny?" I said eagerly.

"Yes," Granny answered in the same absentminded voice, "a waking dream, real as life it seemed, about a flying girl and a boy, and a blackbird as big as a roc . . ." Her voice trailed down into silence.

"But it was all just some nonsense," Granny said suddenly, in the dry efficient voice I associated with bedtime, or the lessons she gave us with woodworking tools. "Soon enough, the end did come. When the factory closed the next week, I looked in my final pay packet and what do you suppose? Along with my usual sixteen bob, there was just an enormous check. The most money I'd ever seen—the most money anyone in my family had seen, back in 1934. With a little note in May Morris's most elegant handwriting: *For the guardian of the Tapestry.*"

Granny suddenly lowered her head to stare at me unblinking. "I doubt you can imagine, children, what that kind of money meant in London, especially in a poor little corner like Pimlico. Charity was a terrible thing my father always said, a terrible thing. But as things were then, well, we couldn't say no. And I am certain"—she paused to give us a surprisingly fierce stare, as if she were looking back through time at her parents—"certain that it was *not* charity. That something was expected for it, something was to be given back."

Granny shifted in her seat, and her eyes again floated up to the ceiling as she put the pictures from the past in their proper order. "That money got us through a decade no one likes to remember too closely. Then eventually, the terrible times ended, the war ended, and one night at a dance up popped your grandfather, fresh from what he called 'the Wild West' and looking smart in a uniform."

"Granny!" Ed said in shocked tones, but I snickered, loving the idea of Granny marrying a man for his beauty. When I think back to Grandpa, he's only a pair of blue eyes and gray hair standing straight up. But back then he was a mechanic for the Army Air Corps, and Granny (this is the one thing I do remember him saying) was his "stolen GI bride."

"Well, he married me in a fortnight," Granny went on, "and took me off to America. And it turned out that nothing in Boston was wild—save the things that taxi drivers would yell at you. Still, I don't think you ever heard me complain."

I didn't say anything, thinking about Grandpa Theo the inventor—"only tinkering," he called it. Ed had a list of every little device that he'd made for Granny over the years, and it was pages long. I loved hearing about the shuttle-rest he'd fastened to one end of her loom, and the little fixed-angle sharpener he'd rigged up for her engraving tools.

"Oh, Theo loved every machine." Granny went on dreamily. "He was always thinking of ways that gears could mesh smoother, or switches fall snug into place. So, between his tinkering and his steady work on the boilers and furnaces downtown, and taking into account my weaving and the classes I taught down at the Bennett Street school, we eventually earned all May's money back, and more.

"Miss Morris herself was long gone by then, but it was as if a voice was speaking to me—I knew just where the money had to go. So, we set out to put every penny of it into collecting all those Arts and Crafts things—some of them English, some of them made over here in Massachusetts, or California. And there was a summer collecting in Norway once, under the midnight sun."

Granny looked around her as if all she'd gathered still sat beneath the Tapestry, instead of tucked away in glass cases in the museum, neatly labeled by Mr. Nazhar. Then she shook herself as if she'd been sleeping,

"Those were the things May and William Morris spent their lives on—and the things they'd spurred others on to make, after them. Putting them back together was what I could do to pay her back somehow. To prove that the Tapestry was safe, and more than safe: that it had a home."

Granny stopped. This was probably the longest story she'd ever told us. I threw myself back with a huge sigh. But she wasn't quite done. "Actually," she began after what must have been a minute, "actually I was young and foolish: Before I let my mother see that check, I slipped back to try to return it, and say a final word to May. But the factory was shut for good. I pounded every door, peeked through every boarded-up window, and found . . . nothing."

"What would you have said, Granny?" put in Ed suddenly. He'd been sitting a little way from us scribbling in his notebook as usual; I hadn't even been sure he was listening. He blushed when we both spun to stare at him. "If you'd found her, I mean."

She didn't hesitate. "I would not have needed many words, Edward. I'd have walked right up to her, tapped my forehead, and said, *What's undone can be done again, Miss Morris.*"

Granny threw herself back in her chair and laughed, and I heard what her fifteen-year-old self must have sounded like. "Well, I was full of myself those days. I do believe I would have put my hand on Miss Morris's arm and said, *You can trust the future to me.*"

The pause in the room stretched and stretched. Mead clicking his beak open and shut and hopping restlessly from perch to perch was the loudest sound in the room. Finally Ed looked up from his notebook expectantly, and I came out with what we'd both been thinking. "So, Granny? Let's hear it!"

"All I can give you to go by," Granny said slowly, "is the words of the poem itself. Somehow the secret's hidden in there, like a set of instructions in a language I don't know. It's all waiting to be unpacked, I'm quite sure—"

"Like computer code!" Ed interrupted her confidently. His head was still leaning against Granny slightly, as if he were drawing energy from her. But his voice was clear and, for him, pretty loud. "Until you find the right machine, computer code—Pascal, or Fortran, or even Basic—just looks like a bunch of sentences, or words, or even letters. When you feed it in to a machine that's set up to listen, though, suddenly it's like a virus unspooling its RNA."

RNA? Virus? I tried to recall if our parents had ever taught us a single thing about science. I had a confused recollection of some dusty magazines on a back shelf in their bedroom, and another image of Ed sitting back there recently, dust bunnies on his jeans from where he'd stuck them under the bed. Still, there he was, suddenly making enough sense about the poem that Granny was stiffening, coming into high-alert mode.

"A code?" she was saying now, softly, puzzling it over. "Yes, I often thought it was a code, certainly. But I always thought that meant I'd have to turn it into something else—"

"Not at all, Granny," interrupted Ed again, jiggling his leg up and down excitedly. "Computer code doesn't need to be translated, it only needs to be *read* the right way. All the instructions are actually in there, waiting to be unlocked. You should give it a try. If we can only find the right machine . . . !" Ed was turning his head this way and that, looking at Mead in his cage, at the walls of the room, at the bookshelves along the far wall, as if some hidden computer was magically going to pop into sight.

I opened my mouth to say that this was not a *Star Trek* episode, and we weren't trapped inside one of those crazy comic books Ed read. But I shut it again. There was something in the air, a kind of electricity.

In fact, there really *was* something in the air. The low rumbling I'd been ignoring was a spring thunderstorm brewing; the air was heavy with rain about to fall. Though it was only late afternoon, the sky had darkened enough that distant lightning flashes made faint flickers across the Tapestry. As the wind stirred it, the animals that hid under its trees almost seemed to be coming to life, winking their eyes and turning to look at us.

I shivered and turned my chair back to where Ed and Granny were sitting quite close to the Tapestry, facing it. As I did, I knocked Mead's cage down. It fell with its usual crash. I may be the best drib-bler and passer on our basketball team, but somehow I still manage to do this about once a week.

The door crashed open and Mead darted out. He never gets far: Our house is tiny and our screens are good. Besides, Granny doesn't really mind his getting a bit of exercise. I tuned out his fluttering—a little more lively than usual, a little frantic even. Granny had taken up her recital position, arms set again for Merton weaving. She cleared her throat and began, her voice light, smooth, and even.

> I am the ancient Apple-Queen,
> For evermore a hope unseen,
> Betwixt the blossom and the bough.
> A gourd and a pilgrim shell, roses dun,
> A ship with shields before the sun.

Granny looked down at this point, and something about our faces made her burst into laughter. "Never seen someone recite a William Morris poem?" she asked drily.

I gulped and nodded. "We recite a poem in English class every month. But those are sonnets usually. And they, well, they, they"—I gulped—"make sense!"

"So does this one," Granny answered promptly. "When you hear it all." On she went.

> A man drew near,
> With painted shield and gold-wrought spear.
> Good was his horse and grand his gear.
> Through the cold garden boughs we went
> Where the tumbling roses shed their scent.

"I still don't get it, Granny," I said, frustration building up inside me and spilling out into my voice, which even to me sounded petu-lant, like a cold and hungry kindergartner, not like a mature eighth grader (virtually a high schooler).

Granny smiled back at me, patient as if we were talking about homework, as if the sky hadn't turned black and thunder hadn't started booming. She went on:

> Therefore Venus well may we
> Praise the green ridges of the sea.

A fork-tongued dragon fresh and fell
Behold I have loved faithfully and well.

Ed yowled pitifully. "Please slow down, Granny!"

She pulled up short, with a little smile. "Guessed its secret yet, Jennie?" she asked with a smile. I hadn't, but I wasn't going to let her see it. Time for a guess.

"It's a puzzle," I began. Then suddenly it came to me. "No, not just a puzzle, a mishmash!"

"Correct," said Granny primly, but I could tell by the corners of her eyes how pleased she was. "It's made up of shreds and patches. 'Dark hills' comes from one of his poems, the 'town of the tree' from another."

She cleared her throat, sat up straight, and went on, her voice rising to give the sense of an ending.

Beside dark hills whose heath-bloom feeds no bee,
All birds sing in the town of the tree.
In the white-flowered hawthorn brake
Love be merry for my sake.
And Thames runs chill
'Twixt mead and hill.

I sat whispering the lines over and over to myself, trying to get it all in there; "*Queen,*" I muttered for the second time, "*unseen.*"

Ed, curled around his notebook, was doing the same. "You might say that poem is woven," Granny went on musingly, "just like the Tapestry. What I always wondered is why May would have chosen the bits she did." She trailed off, gazing absently at one of the largest of the Lost Spots, a huge threadless swatch right in the middle of a green wave-tossed sea.

"Again, Granny!" demanded Ed suddenly, not looking up from his notebook. Without comment, she began again at the beginning: "I am the ancient Apple-Queen," she said, this time almost shouting. "For evermore a hope unseen." I found it hard to focus. The wind was rising outside almost to a howl, and lightning was flashing every few seconds.

"Ed," I shouted, trying to break the daze he'd fallen into. "We shouldn't let Mead fly around in weather like this. He's acting crazy!"

Instead of banging against the windows as usual, Mead kept circling nearer and nearer to the tapestry, almost touching it. He kept returning to one spot in the lower left-hand corner, where a meadow turned into a hill, and a blue river snaked away into the distance. There was a wagon filled with barrels creaking across the river at that point, so life-like you could almost hear the burly driver roaring at his oxen. One of the Lost Spots was in that part of the tapestry, too, a pair of triangles and a squiggle I'd often puzzled over.

Ed and I usually trapped Mead by spreading our arms wide and finally pinning him against some handy flat surface. As we crept forward now, preparing for the moment when we both lunged at once, I could hear Granny, slow and loud and careful, like someone casting a spell, reciting the poem's final lines:

And Thames runs chill
'Twixt mead and hill.

And as she finished saying "hill," three things happened at once.

First, Ed and I both leapt toward Mead, who was fluttering just beyond our grasp, right up against the Tapestry (but our leap was too strong, we were going to smash into the wall!). Second, there was a low booming sound, like faraway thunder. Third, I smelled something like a hot summer rain: damp, and a little whiff of sulfur like lightning had just struck. Before I had time to think about that smell, or what it meant that Ed and I had been falling toward the tapestry for quite a while but hadn't yet smacked our skulls on the wall behind it, I stopped noticing anything at all.

CHAPTER THREE

Betwixt the Blossom
and the Bough

Okay, *fine*, I was thinking in the slowed-down way they say comes with crashes, *okay I'm falling, falling but not landing.* I opened my eyes, and shut them again immediately, because what I saw made no sense.

In that quick glimpse I saw a riverside meadow, and a hill, and not far off a man in a leather vest driving an old-fashioned wagon over a bridge. Near him, galloping on a fat little pony, was a kid wearing armor and waving a sword over his head. Though I couldn't place it exactly, I knew this place, knew it very well.

What made me squeeze my eyes shut and scream "Ed!" in a squeaky voice was *how* I was seeing all this. From above. Way, way above, like the blimp's-eye view of Fenway Park they sometimes show on TV.

36

"Yeah, Jen?" came an eager voice right behind me. "Have you checked out the view? *So* awesome! I knew that poem was a code! The Tapestry must have been the machine; that's what May must have been doing with the poem, somehow setting up this program so that we could . . ."

"Oh great, thanks for the briefing, Einstein!" I said as ferociously as I could muster between panicky gasps. Any minute now, I was definitely going to open my eyes. "Do you have any idea where we are, Ed?"

"Well," he said immediately, "we might be in England to judge by the meadows, and that wagon, and the rain, and the costume that boy down there is—"

I cut him off. "No, I mean where? Where! Are we inside a helicopter, or a plane that's going down, or . . ."

My voice trailed off; Ed had reached forward to grab my waist. "Relax, sis," he said soothingly as if he had the best news you've heard all day, "I know exactly where we are. We're just riding around on Mead's back."

"Oh good," I said automatically.

Then my eyes snapped open. Nope, not good at all. I shut them again. After a moment, I reached out a hand gingerly to feel around in front of me: It definitely felt like feathers, each one as long as my forearm. I took a deep breath and opened my eyes to find myself staring at the back of Mead's head. He clicked his beak in what might have been a friendly hello.

Five minutes ago Mead had been the ordinary kind of blackbird who could land on your wrist if he felt like it. How could we possibly be gliding through the air with nothing but him between us and a gruesome, extremely messy death?

Looking around, I saw that Ed was balancing behind me by leaning against Mead's upturned tail, which was a little bit bigger than the back of a comfy armchair. That wasn't going to work for me, but while my mind was still freaking out my body had figured out the trick. My knees were gripping tight right above Mead's wings. Sitting on Mead was kind of like riding a feather-covered horse, except that where you'd want to slide your legs down and feel for stirrups, there was nothing but wing.

I was trying to get up my courage to have a good look at the new Mead (*just super-sized, nothing but super-sized*, I told myself). When I did look forward, I caught him looking back at me at exactly the same time: I'd never noticed how bright and yellow a blackbird's eyes could be.

Ed had apparently adjusted quicker than I had to life in the air. "Hey, Jen," he called, pointing down into the far end of the field, where shadows were falling long and velvety gray. "Who's that fat little boy on the pony?"

I looked down hard at the kid; focusing on something on the ground made me feel a lot less scared, I noticed. I've always had a good eye for faces, so without thinking I called out, "William Morris!"

Then I stopped, confused. "Well, I mean if the kid were a grown-up with a red beard, and we were in nineteenth-century England—which we're obviously *not*!"

Ed just snorted. "Yeah, and we're not flying on Mead's back."

And without taking the time to think about it, or consult his note-book for directions, Ed all of sudden started yelling, "William, yoo-hoo, O Willy! I have this Tapestry to ask you about!"

At which point Mead, who'd been flapping us steadily closer to the meadow, cleared his throat and looked back over his shoulder, exactly as if he were going to speak to us. We both shot him a quick glance, then went back to staring at William Morris. So he cleared his throat again.

I looked back at him, with the friendly face I always use for puppies, or cats that I think might let me pet them. "Good boy, Mead!" I said chirpily, or at least what I think of as chirpily. And Ed chimed in, "Want a cracker, Mead?"

Mead opened his beak and closed it. Glared at us. Then opened it again and said in one of those "propah" English accents from old movies, clear as day, "Thank you, Ed, no. I don't very much want a cracker."

Someday scientists will discover that among human instincts, the strongest of all is the desire to humiliate your sister. Before we had time to scream, or get air sickness, or even think about what all this might mean, Ed turned to me and muttered, "Oh yeah, Jen, we're not in nineteenth-century England—and Mead did *not* just talk to us in a Mary Poppins voice."

And with that, he turned back and started yelling down again. "Yoo-hoo, excuse me, William; the Tapestry I need to ask you about is mostly blue and gold, with designs of . . . Huh! Hey, Mead"—Ed

leaned forward indignantly, as if he'd been complaining to blackbirds his whole life—"why is William Morris ignoring us?"

By this time Morris, or at least the fat little kid on the pony, was already almost in the forest. At the last minute, though, he glanced briefly overhead, and suddenly pulled his pony up short, making it rear in a very cowboy-movie kind of way. Seeing a giant bird, he drew his sword, waved it ferociously, and shouted at the top of his lungs, "Yoicks!"

Then he galloped out of sight. I heard a sound like two dry old boulders rubbing together, and realized that Mead was chuckling. Chuckling at us. "Dear me!" he said gravely. "Dear me! I do believe you've been challenged to a duel by a schoolboy!"

We were left staring after him in dismay. About ten thousand questions ran through my head: Where was our house? What had happened when we crashed into the tapestry? Why were we on Mead's back? How were we going to get home? I opened my mouth to begin and instead found myself saying, in a humble voice I barely recognized as my own, "Mead, do you suppose we could find a nice place to land? A place where we could talk for a minute?"

Rather than answer, Mead turned his face back toward us again. Blackbird or no, I recognized his expression from basketball. I'd seen it on the face of a point guard who got the ball ten points behind with only three minutes to play. *I can still do this*, that look says, *I can do it, but only if absolutely everything goes right.*

Something about Mead's face made me spin my head around to see if something was chasing us. Nothing there; but I did see one of Mead's tail-feathers tumbling slowly down to the meadow below. That wasn't normal, was it?

Then it hit me; that meadow! "It's on the Tapestry," I shouted triumphantly. "This is the meadow on the Tapestry! I recognize that oak forest, and the river down there, and . . ." Ed was just opening his mouth to interrupt me when Mead suddenly dropped, absolutely dropped out of the sky. He fell like a rock or a meteorite (a feathery meteorite) and both of us screamed. As we plunged toward the edge of the forest Morris had just entered, Mead said—now sounding more like an excited game-show contestant—"Ooo, what a nice-looking apple, down there betwixt the blossom and the bough!"

With that, Mead entered the forest at top speed and neatly clawed an apple off the tree. Just like that, we were back up the sky, heading straight for a huge gray cloud bank. I squeezed as tight as I could with my knees. Sliding off those slippery black feathers, Ed had no choice but to grab at my bag awkwardly—I heard the seams groaning. Far away as it was, the whirling ground below still managed to look awfully hard and stony.

Ed was screaming, "Hey, Mead, where are you taking us? Mead? Mead?!" But as we plunged into the heavy storm cloud that loomed above us I was trying to think where I'd heard "betwixt the blossom and the bough" before.

CHAPTER FOUR

facts, facts, facts

e came out of the cloud above a glowing white spire. Not that far above: Mead's claw imme‑ diately banged into the very tip, and both of us jolted upright, holding on extremely tight. I heard him mutter something that sounded like "*Obese grandchildren*" (I must have heard wrong . . .).

"Land, please!" Ed snapped; he was frantically trying to hold on to a notebook that was about to get away from him. I heard Mead mutter again, more faintly. But after a minute he did spin in a tight circle ("Ooo, rats; I mean Yoicks!" Ed yelped, as two pens tumbled out of his pocket) and bring us to a neat landing atop the spire. I took a breath and began to look around.

We were no longer in the countryside; now we were in the middle of a town, maybe even a little city. All around us were tight coils of streets, with apartment buildings and row houses interspersed with little cottages and stand-alone houses blended in. Down below us the traffic (on the left side of the road, I noticed) was a mixture of country carts, fancy horse-drawn carriages, and the occasional mounted man or woman. The building we were on was by far the tallest in sight, and as far as I could make sense of it from above, it was a medieval-looking cathedral.

I thought about other people I knew who'd ridden birds: the only one who came to mind was Sinbad riding the roc in the Arabian Nights, and I couldn't remember how that had ended up. Not well, probably.

Ed yelped suddenly and pointed down to the entrance of the cathedral. There, accompanied by a pair of very parental-looking people (her silk umbrella, his walking stick and fussy top hat), I caught sight of the kid William Morris, still in Ivanhoe-style armor, complete with wooden sword—although he'd apparently left the pony at home. Ed immediately started yelling again. "Yoo-hoo, William Morris, about that tapestry . . ."

Mead sounded more like Mary Poppins than ever. "Erhemmm-mmm, Edward, a bit of brain power, please. He's still only nine. As a matter of fact today is the day that he's first been brought to see Canterbury Cathedral and its beautiful illuminated books."

"Wait, you mean Canterbury as in Chaucer's *Canterbury Tales?*" said Ed in a genuinely impressed voice. Mead nodded smugly, as if he'd built it himself.

All of a sudden, I was incredibly exasperated with them both. "Ed, until we know what exactly is going on, do me a favor and stop scream-ing at Morris! Would you really like all those people down there to look up and notice us riding on the back of a giant bird?" Ed turned toward me belligerently and opened his mouth to say something; then paused, thought better of it, looked down at the ground without speaking.

"Okay," I said. I tapped on Mead's head (and felt another feather slide off his shoulder). "Listen, can you *please* stop proving you're the smartest bird in the room and tell us what exactly is going on? I think you know a lot more than us"—Mead gave a triumphant nod when I said this. "But" I went on, "I also imagine you need us as much as we need you. Otherwise, we wouldn't be here, would we?"

At this, Mead clicked his beak indignantly then, almost exactly like Ed, looked down at the ground in thought. I waited a second to make sure he had nothing more to say.

"Here's what I can figure." I let them hear my anger, and my fear as well. "Something happened when Granny was reciting the Tapestry poem, right?"

Ed bounced up and down approvingly and smiled—he was on the same page with me. But I was studying Mead, whose face was now turned away in profile. Like a dog that knows you're keeping an eye on him, he was pretending to ignore me, but I knew he was listen-ing. After a second he nodded.

"So when the poem ended, the Tapestry . . ." I paused, not sure I had the right word for what had happened. "It . . ."

"It opened for me," said Mead. "As I've always known it would."

"For us!" said Ed immediately. "It opened for us!"

"Only because you were touching me!" Mead snapped at him, a little shiver of indignation running through his body and making us both squeeze our knees tighter.

I took a deep breath; this was all starting to come together. "Mead?" I asked cautiously, keeping my voice polite and light. "Have you ever tried to enter the Tapestry before?"

He looked at me guardedly for a minute and then nodded. "As long as I've been with your grandmother, I've known that I was meant to. But it never opened up before today."

"Because it was only today she said the poem?" I suggested.

Mead started to nod, then stopped. "No," he said in a voice that sounded less cranky, more puzzled. "She's said it before: The night your grandfather died, she said it with her hand on the meadow, said it over and over. The day of the crash, too, she stood there reciting and crying, crying and reciting, until night fell."

He looked me straight in the eye. "Nothing. Nothing ever happened until today."

The wind was fairly high on the tower—I could tell we couldn't stay there forever without losing our grip. But I had to ask Mead one more thing. "Do you suppose," I said carefully, "that we belong to your quest, too, whatever it is? That our touching you wasn't an accident, that it was the point?"

He stared at me a long time, as if he were trying to read my mind. Rather than say anything, he very slowly brought up from underneath him his right claw. The move made us slide off the spire suddenly, and just like that we were aloft.

I realized with a start, though, that the claw wasn't empty: he was holding out to me the thing he'd snatched from "betwixt the blossom and the bough": a single glowing apple that fell into my open palm. I can't imagine my expression at that moment. For some reason, though, my mind shot back to the face of the girl on the Tapestry, the one grasping for that empty space where an apple should be. I wondered for just an instant what her face looked like now.

For the first time since we'd gotten the letter from the museum that morning I allowed a small feeling of triumph to spread through my chest and warm me. I tucked the apple carefully in the basketball bag and turned to Ed with a smile.

"What's the poem say after *bough*?" I asked him. And without even glancing down at his notebook, as if he was expecting me to ask that very question, Ed recited:

> *A gourd and a pilgrim shell, roses dun,*
> *A ship with shields before the sun.*

As Ed finished speaking, Mead was already diving toward a line of people in very old-fashioned getup filing slowly out of the cathedral. We barreled closer, the distance to the ground telescoping minute by minute, details snapping into focus. One of those pilgrims had around her neck a water-gourd, with a scallop shell tied to its neck.

I was dazzled by how deftly Mead managed to grab the little

gourd and shell just before we pulled out of our dive and headed for the clouds again. It was too bad the pilgrim stayed firmly attached.

$\mathcal{A}$s Mead brought us through another cloud bank, and out over a town dotted with pointed spires and steep tile roofs, a regular cloud of feathers fell loose from his tail. I counted nine as they spiraled lazily down below us. Looking up from my counting I caught Mead, too, watching them go.

"What's his rush?" I whispered. Ed looked up in surprise when I said that. Then after a long pause he nodded and made a note. It was something Granny had taught him to do when I asked him any-thing about feelings. "Your sister reads faces the way you read math books," I remember her telling Ed, "and she can find a whole opera's worth of drama in a single expression she glimpses in passing. Until you can look someone in the eye long enough to figure out what he really wants, Ed, you listen to her when she tells you about a face."

I don't think I would have known that about me and faces if Granny hadn't said it. But she was right. I usually knew who was going to yell at the teacher before the teacher—sometimes it even seemed like I knew before the yeller did. And I could pretty much walk into a room and sense who was mad at the kid in the next desk, and who was about to go to sleep. "You smell it!" Ed said once accusingly. You would have thought that kind of face reading might help me with Eva, and her friends—but somehow it didn't work that way.

When Mead looked me full in the face, though, all he said was,

"Tuck this away somewhere, there's a good girl." He passed me the shell and gourd, now minus their pilgrim (I caught a glimpse of her in a lake below, indignantly dog-paddling toward shore). I found room for them in my gym bag while Mead floated us down to a flat-roofed old building. We landed disturbingly near an edge, perched just above a pair of open windows.

Still, it was better than nothing. For the first time I felt comfortable sliding off Mead's back and stretching my legs. While Ed headed off to see what he could spy over the edge, I dug out the water bottle and a big box of granola bars I always kept stashed in the bottom of my gym bag. Below that I glimpsed only a couple of withered apples. But we'd definitely be home before we needed those.

"Here," I said, diffidently offering the box. "I think that top one may have some sunflower seeds." As he dug eagerly into the bar I felt my back shake all over: Mead had thumped me with his wing, a real thank-you thump. I felt another warm glow; not exactly triumph but something a little deeper, and harder to classify.

I lay down for a minute, closed my eyes, and took three deep breaths. Opened them again and there I still was, on a rooftop that was definitely dirty enough to be in England, and 160 years old. There really was no way I could find to make it add up. Ed was happily scribbling in his notebook, I noticed, probably calculating years traveled per minute, or the ratio of Mead's body weight to our velocity, or some other set of numbers that would make a nice chart. But it was the big picture I kept stumbling over. When Ed and I read *The Hobbit* together as kids, he had a whole series of questions: How could something as big as a dragon fly? When you're invisible can you see yourself? Are wizards originally humans or are they another race? What about their mothers? And so on. Me, I only had one question: Where is this place? When Granny asked me if I wanted to go there, I always shook my head stubbornly. It wasn't that. I just needed to know if Middle Earth was a place I might end up sometime, if it *could* happen.

Well, something finally had happened. So I should be the happy one—but it was Ed who was humming to himself. Somehow the first thing that came to mind was what this all had to do with all the fantasy games we'd played over the years. Ed liked it when we played at being Captain Kirk and Dr. Spock, but my favorite game was called Fantastic Voyage. Riding a tiny submarine inside somebody's veins appealed to me way more than barrelling through space a zillion miles from home.

"Since we're along for the ride, Mead"—Ed's voice snapped me back to our roof—"maybe we can—"

"Maybe you can tell me," Mead cut in gruffly, "if you know anything useful about the Tapestry that got us into this mess."

"Well," said Ed, flipping back excitedly through his notebook, "I can tell you about William Morris. He was born just north of London, in 1834. He grew up riding around Epping Forest"—he flipped a page—"wearing a little suit of medieval armor and imagining that he was Ivanhoe."

"I can tell you more than that," I broke in. "Along with Leonardo and Thomas Edison, he's Granny's hero. She told us that when we make stencils, or design window tracings, or even try to make wood-blocks for wallpaper, we're learning to make art the way he did."

Ed cut me off again. "If you really, really want something in your house, you ought to know how to make it yourself. The first one you make isn't going to be as beautiful as you had your heart set on, and probably the second or third or even the fourth won't be, either. But maybe the fifth!"

I held up my hands for Mead to inspect. "So you see, that's why I have this cut over here—that's from a chisel. And this little scar here is only from hot wax—Granny says we're lucky it wasn't molten glass. And this finger bends back funny because one day my stencil tool slipped and . . ."

Finger in his notebook, Ed cut me off, slipping into the routine I secretly call *the computer wore sneakers:* "Morris and his Company designed or helped to design amazing new kinds of furniture, glassware, stained glass, tiles, wallpaper—that was very popular!—rugs, printed books, and, oh yes, tapestries. Plus"— blushing a little—"I think there are more but I kind of squashed a brownie onto my list."

Mead gave a little wing-flirt; a shrug. "Facts, facts, facts!" he suddenly grated out. "My goodness, Edward, what are you planning to do with all of them; open a shop?" Ed stared back at him blankly, as if Mead had asked him what he was going to do with his heart, stomach, and kidneys.

I started to rise to Ed's defense, but Mead kept talking in the sort of creaky crabby voice I associated with the old guy ahead of you in line at the store, who just knows that his senior discount card is in here somewhere if you could give him a minute, for Pete's sake

"I didn't bring you here to lecture me about the birth of Arts and Crafts," Mead went on. "I'm sure you do enough of that to your schoolmasters." I suppressed a snort; I had seen the slightly glazed eyes of Ed's photography teacher the day Ed started talking about Emery Walker and photogravure techniques in the 1880s. Mead was running one claw hurriedly across his breast, as if he were ironing his feathers back in place. "Don't you two realize that we haven't much time? Not much time at all before—" He stopped abruptly.

"Before what, Mead?" Then I had a sudden thought. "Mead," I started to ask, "do your feathers have—"

"Before," he went on in a louder voice, "we finish decoding this mysterious poem." There went the feather below his right eye. He watched me watching it fall, then we both turned our heads to watch Ed make a tally mark in his notebook. "Twenty-six, minimum," Ed said audibly, but seemingly to himself. Mead and I looked at each other warily; did we want to know what Ed thought it meant that this was the twenty-sixth feather Mead had lost? A pause. No.

So quickly that Mead probably missed it, Ed threw me a glance. Sometimes our brother-sister telepathy kicks in at moments like this. When it does, it's always my job to say whatever we're thinking.

"Mead," I began humbly. Everyone knows I can out-humble Ed; it's one reason we're such a good team. "There's obviously something we need to know." Mead was nodding approvingly as I said this.

Unfortunately, I went on. "And I bet there's something William Morris needs, too, if we can only find out what it is."

At this, Mead glared indignantly and gave what would have been an extremely loud squawk if he hadn't managed to cut if off after the first *Sqw—*. "What *He* needs?" Mead said. "What *He* needs is what great artists always need. He needs—" The two of us were silent; Ed had his pencil poised. Mead, though, only glared and harrumphed (something I'd only read about in books before, but when Mead harrumphed there was no mistaking it).

"What Morris needs will, I hope, become apparent to you as we go along," he said. It seemed to be his last word on the subject.

There was a long pause and then I said, "Well, since I won that poetrymemorizing contest last year, I guess it's my job to say that we are now officially looking for 'roses dun' and 'a ship with shields before the sun.'"

Mead gave me another of those little wing buffets, which had the scary effect of pushing me a lot closer to the edge of the roof, and the open windows below us. "That," he said briskly, "is the most sensible thing you've said this morning. Join your sister above that window, Ed, and let's see what we can hear."

As he bullied us forward, Mead cleared his throat and added, "Err, I suppose you need to know a few more, err, um . . ."

Ed, head still down, but with a sneaky smile, muttered, "A few facts, Mead?"

"Details," said Mead stiffly, "pertinent historical details is what you'd like to hear now. It matters to you that William Morris headed off in 1852 to Oxford University. And it matters that right away he found himself a lifelong friend, Edward Burne-Jones. That he also picked out his first true teacher: the art historian John Ruskin."

Even though Mead kept talking, I had a hard time concentrating, and I noticed that I'd started to get goose bumps. Because underneath his rumble I could hear something from inside: a husky but highly enthusiastic voice saying "Oh my dear Burne-Jones, it's so good to find someone else who loves churches, and the Middle Ages, and most of all John Ruskin!"

Peeping in, we could see it was unmistakably an almost grown-up version of the boy who'd yelled "Yoicks" at us. He busily hoisting into place above his bed a slightly terrifying bust. It depicted the sort of bearded professor who looked like he regularly spoke with the President—or with God.

His roommate, who was stroking an amazingly long and wispy beard for such a young man, glanced nervously up at the bust. "Err, yes," he said dubiously. "Yes, quite quite . . . He's, err, well he's very, ummmmmmm . . ."

Burne-Jones never got beyond "ummmmmmmmm"; Morris was waving his arms around enthusiastically, getting a bit red in the face. "Yes, you're absolutely right, absolutely right; isn't he just? Thanks to Ruskin I finally understand what it means for each of us to labor passionately at what we love doing, and to strive to make our own corner of the world beautiful. Ruskin's love of handicraft has persuaded me to give up on being a priest, and instead to become . . ."

Ed, unable to resist, poked his head through the open window at this moment and blurted out, "A tapestry weaver!"

I yanked him back out, and Mead dropped right off the ledge. As we zoomed away I heard Morris finishing his sentence, ". . . an architect." Then, after a very short pause, "I say, Ned old thing, did you hear a ruckus outside? Or a rumpus?"

CHAPTER FIVE

Girl of the Ledge

**W**ell, 1852 doesn't seem to be our year, does it?" said Mead irritably. "May I recommend a little less talk next time, Edward—and a little more burglary!"

By this point, we were already circling back toward what looked like the same heavy gray cloud we'd dropped from. I watched with concern as feathers—three, four, five of them—flicked free from the underside of his left wing. We wobbled and lurched suddenly, dropping for a moment before resuming our shaky climb.

"Mead?" Those feathers.

"If I can manage this next flight right, we might want to try for December 1855." Mead had a neat knack for ignoring what he didn't want to talk about. I heard a crisp "Now hold tight!" A little tunnel opened up in the bottom of that ponderous cumulus cloud, and in we went. For a second I had that same misty feeling you get when you walk into the bathroom while someone else is showering. After that, a tug. More than a tug really, as if a giant had taken hold of me from two directions and yanked me apart, just for a second, then let me slap back into one piece. We were banking out of the clouds again; I shot a look over at Ed to see if he felt as awful as me. Head bent over his notebook, he was adding up a column of numbers with a frown.

I recognized the spires and the river instantly—except for an eerie sense that the southern horizon had changed (a dome less, a factory more?), it was the same town. "Oxford!" I shouted quickly, just for the pleasure of beating Mead to it: He closed his beak with an irritated snap. The window ledge we landed on, though, was broader, almost a miniature balcony, and the room we glimpsed behind a set of velvet curtains (a beautiful blue-gray, like a cat's back) was considerably fancier than Morris's last. As Ed and I cautiously sidled forward off Mead's back, he cleared his throat.

"When he graduated Oxford with Ned Burne-Jones, Morris had, err, errrr, taken on a new nickname: Topsy." He paused for a moment, daring us to giggle. When we kept silent, he gave a brief nod and said, "You'll have recognized the reference to the curly-haired heroine of Uncle Tom's Cabin?"

I kept my face politely blank, a trick I'd learned while listening to Ed talk about photogravure. After a moment Mead went on.

"Well, Morris and Burne-Jones graduated knowing only two things for certain: that they loved the Middle Ages, and that they were art-ists. Morris was a hero-worshipper in those days, and he picked an unlikely set of heroes."

Ed, pencil at the ready, clearly wanted to know about those heroes: I didn't need to glance over to know that he already had a page labeled PERTINENT DETAILS and a neatly ruled column, MORRIS HEROES. For me, though, there was something more important to clear up first.

"Mead?" I whispered urgently. "This is starting to feel all weird, like a video game. Is this . . ." I trailed off, not sure what I meant to say. "I mean, I'm actually here? Not in a hospital bed with a concussion. Not inside somebody else's dreams. Really in Oxford in 1855?"

Mead stared at me for a second. Then very gingerly he reached a claw sideways and poked a tiny bundle on the ledge next to me, something I hadn't noticed. It twitched indignantly and waved some feelers furiously up at Mead. He put his head right near it, mouth wide, seemingly about to swallow it whole. Then he reconsidered and turned back to me with a sigh. The beetle scurried quickly in my direction and disappeared behind my hip.

"Well, I find I can't eat it, after all." Noticing my blank gaze, he tsssked indignantly. "You don't recognize the Blue Stag Beetle, then?" I shook my head dumbly. "Don't know that industrial pollu-tion killed it off in Great Britain in 1860?" Again I shook my head. "Goodness, me, what do they teach . . ." Mead trailed off with a sad little set of clicks, like an engine running down. The claw that he waved feebly in a gesture of dismissal seemed to indicate he wasn't going to be able to prove anything to me, after all.

As I crept forward, I realized that Mead's entomology lesson had actually worked. The Blue Stag Beetle, which was really more of a dusty gray, had convinced me that wherever we were was filled with creatures that ate, breathed, slept, waved their antennae.

But none of this wondering was getting me anywhere. *Remember you have a poem and something you're supposed to do,* I told myself sternly. I clutched my gym bag tighter and tried to stop worrying about Mead's feathers. It would probably turn out to be nothing at all, some kind of mange. Did birds actually get mange, or was that only stuffed animals in books? I'd have to ask Ed.

I hurried to catch up with the other two, who'd managed to creep farther along the windowsill. Peeping cautiously in through a crack in Morris's velvet curtains, I saw faded old carpets everywhere, including one that had been fastened not just to a wall but also to the ceiling, so that its giant primroses, flowering vines, and peacocks loomed over Morris and Ned as they sat together scribbling. Ned was drawing tall soulful ladies in medieval gowns.

By keeping myself concealed behind the drapes as I moved I could practically touch the table where Morris sat writing, a grown man now, with a red beard covering a faintly noticeable double chin. He was scratching away furiously—humming, but also grumbling and fidgeting and tossing away pieces of paper at a great rate. I found that I was whispering "roses dun" and "ship with shields before the sun" under my breath over and over, like a magic spell. Which in a way it was.

I could just hear Morris saying: "Well, my dear Ned, what's the good of all this family money if I can't spend it? Whereas if I do throw it around a bit, we can get all those marvelous artists from London to come up and work with us. The Pre-Raphaelite Brotherhood, they call themselves. Besides, doesn't that title page look grand?" He pointed up at an elegant light blue page stuck to the wall with *The Oxford and Cambridge Magazine* outlined in bold letters.

Ned hemmed and stroked his beard. "Yes, well, but Topsy, I'm not sure if throwing money at people is the best way to—"

"Yes, yes, splendid! I knew you'd see it my way!" broke in Morris cheerily, tipping over one of Ned's long bottles of inks with his sleeve (Ned caught it before a drop spilled).

"I've already written to the most famous of the lot, William Holman Hunt," Morris went on rapidly. "It was his painting *The Awakening Conscience* that sent a shock through me when I first saw it—like a novel come to life! I imagine his friends in the brotherhood will accompany him to Oxford. And I'm sure they'll be delighted to hear about our grave rubbings, and these marvelous little French copper roses we found . . . almost dun-colored, aren't they?"

I heard a bell tinkle faintly below. As Morris and Ned stepped toward the doorway, I felt Mead nudging my back. Almost without stopping to think about it, I launched my body out from behind the drapes and through the window, half toppling inward.

As Ned turned back into the room, I grabbed blind for one of the dun roses. I was a second too late; my fingers scraped against it and it rolled tantalizingly away just as Morris burst through the doorway. Now the room was filling up with people; I looked despairingly back at Ed, and Mead crouched behind me. *Wait till they leave?* I mouthed at Ed and he shrugged. *No choice!* he mouthed back. Mead turned his head away without comment; I saw a tiny neck feather give way.

Trying not to think about Mead's possible mange, I tucked my head back into the convenient spot I'd found behind the velvet curtain. Ed was apparently still clamoring for "pertinent details," because after a series of hisses and a rustle of feathers that I associated with Mead shaking his head, I heard him say in a low voice, "Well, look it up when you get home, Edward. You'll find the Pre-Raphaelites loved the intense color and complex natural world they found in paintings by Giotto, Botticelli, and Leonardo, not to mention Raphael. It was just before him that they felt Italian art had reached its apex—" Long pause. "—its acme—" Longer pause. "—oh for heaven's sake, its apogee, its telos, its, its, its height, you little featherless ninny!"

I stifled a chuckle. It occurred to me that I'd be grumpy, too, if I were saddled with two ignoramuses on a quest that I'd always dreamed of accomplishing myself.

That was it! I gave such a jerk of surprise that anyone looking at the drapes at that moment would have thought a piece of lumber had suddenly fallen against them. Mead was treating us the way he was because *he* had wanted to be the hero who saved the Tapestry—and then we showed up.

When I turned back to share my discovery, Ed shushed me violently. Inside the room, Morris was fumbling all over himself to make the introductions.

"Mr. John Everett Millais, may I present Edward Burne-Jones? Like me, Ned is an admirer of your recent painting of Ophelia. She's a marvelous corpse. I mean to say, she's so wonderfully, beautifully, errr, thoroughly dead!"

Burne-Jones stepped forward, bowed with more dignity than I'd been expecting, and said, without a stutter or a stammer, "Mr. Millais, your painting of *Christ in the House of His Parents* was a revelation to me. The way you painted Jesus the Lord as a common child of the laboring classes, his bald father's dusty apron, the wood shavings, well, sir . . . !"

Ned's nerve deserted him at this point; he turned bright red and jerked to a stop like a windup toy. Nonetheless, I saw Millais give a slight involuntary bow in return, and study the younger artist's face carefully. As for Morris, he looked at Ned the way you might look at a checker if it suddenly made its own move. He laughed and poked Ned hard in the ribs. Without missing a beat, Ned poked him right back.

"Come along, Neddy, let me present you to the beard, err I mean the man you've no doubt long admired, William Hunt." (Morris was right: This guy's beard looked like a giant orange tomcat sleeping on his chest.) "Sir," boomed Morris energetically, "your painting *The Hireling Shepherd*, with its pert shepherdess—yes, oh yes, so unrestrained, so frank, so delightfully sensual . . ."

All at once Morris subsided. Dressed in rumpled painter's smock and corduroy trousers with smears of violet and green, the final Pre-Raphaelite somehow managed to make the room itself look badly dressed. He immediately reminded me of Principal Hirsh at my junior high school. Somehow he always managed to let everyone know that the moment he walked in the door was the perfect time for the real business of the day to begin.

Although everyone had fallen totally silent, he suavely finished the point he had been making on the stairway. "So you see, I suggested we take the name *Pre-Raphaelites* so that we should never forget the Italian masters and the way the tiniest weed in the corner of their sketch threatens to burst into bloom. The so-called Renaissance that came after them was mechanical, artificial—and deplorably commercial."

Morris rushed forward. "Oh Ned, allow me: the great Dante Gabriel Rossetti."

"Very good." Rossetti inclined his head graciously. "Did you say you had ordered up some champagne wine for us, err, Mr., err . . ." His voice trailed off absently as he looked around, taking in the drawings by Ned that coated every available surface.

Morris hurried to pass around glasses, still chattering. "Indeed, the Pre-Raphaelite principles have been most inspiring to us, haven't they, Ned? But surely, Mr. Rossetti—may I call you Gabriel?—you meant that the Renaissance went astray in how it treated its workers?" Rossetti, who had found a champagne glass and was busily

filling it, looked around as if the treatment of workers in the Renaissance had been the very last thing on his mind.

Morris plowed on undaunted (*He's probably 100 percent
undauntable,* I thought). "It was the free workers of the Middle
Ages, after all, whose illustrated books still freeze us in our tracks,
with their remarkable combination of fantastical invention and truth
to nature. What are we as artists if we fail to study nature, to devour
her? Take, for example"—looking around nervously, anxious to make
a good impression—"that most peculiar and absolutely enormous
bird that's peeking at us from that window . . ." His voice trailed off.

"Good Lord, Ned! Don't be a dunce, snare it, snare it!" Morris
jumped up, dousing Rossetti with champagne. Ed scrambled awkwardly onto Mead's back as he tumbled off the ledge, but I wasn't
so lucky. They were away through the air before I could grab hold,
and Morris, flinging back the velvet curtain, was glaring right at me.

I stared back at him wide-eyed. Nothing happened for a minute, long enough for me to notice the random noise below: heavy
shoes clicking on pavement, the muffled clatter of a doorbell. Then,
rather than yelling, or grabbing hold of me, Morris inclined his head
and shoulders forward through the window, letting the curtain fall
behind him. He was smiling.

"Well, well, not a roc at all, but a girl!" he said finally. "The
sort who's not afraid to clamber across ledges to find something she
wants." He paused, looked me carefully in the eyes. He must have
seen something of what we'd been going through, or maybe smelled
it on me. The tears, the desperation, even something about Granny.

Whatever it was, his smile changed slightly, deepened maybe, as his face seemed to grow brighter red.

"No, I beg your pardon," he said at last, fumbling around for something in one of his deep pockets. "To find something she *needs* . . . is that right?"

Trembling with fear, I nodded dumbly. And Morris, too, fell silent. As if it were the most ordinary thing in the world to find a total stranger perched on your fifth-story window ledge, he looked at me appraisingly. Without a word he pulled something out of his pocket and handed it to me. I could only gaze into his eyes and try desperately not to scream.

Morris finally did break the spell. "I think," he said gravely, no hint of teasing in his voice, "that I recognize the look of one under a *geas*. Have you anything to tell me, Girl of the Ledge? Any message that you'd wish me to hear?"

It was the kind of moment you dream about—what would you tell Leonardo, what would you ask Michelangelo? Ed would probably order Morris to get to work weaving. But I could let him know how much he meant to Granny, and how hard Mr. Nazhar was working to save everything he'd made. Or just ask him what exactly a geas was.

"What's undone will be done!" I blurted out suddenly, surprising myself almost as much as him. Morris's eyes widened; he opened his mouth to respond—and I felt myself suddenly lifted into the air by my right shoulder. Then I was falling, almost floating through the air, flailing, yelping—before Mead fastened his other claw on my gym bag.

I just had time to hear Morris's delighted cry: "I knew there was a roc,

by God!" Then Mead's downward trajectory took us shooting between a pair of onrushing willows and ("Hold your breath!" Mead managed to pant out) the green water of the Thames came up to slap us. As it did, I heard a tearing sound, right near the shoulder Mead held me by. The water was too strong, and my basketball jacket had never been built for this. As the seam gave, I started to slip away. I opened my mouth to scream, but water filled it. I was in the Thames, really in it, sinking fast and Mead was—I flailed around frantically—where *was* Mead?

"Ed!" I tried to scream when I broke the surface, but got only another mouthful of water. I came up again, and seemed to have plenty of time to take in the horrified expression of the two students in the punt near me. Time enough even to notice that nearly empty bottle of champagne one of them was clutching.

"Going down for the third time," I heard a voice—was it Granny's?—saying, over and over. As I went down, though, I felt a rush of air and sensed something plummeting through the open air toward me. Eyes closed and head already underwater, I grabbed desperately with my left hand at whatever was above me. With two fingers and a slippery thumb, I clung like death to the thin scaly rod, trying not to think about the horrible crunching sound I'd heard as my fingers closed on what had to be Mead's leg.

"Duck, Jerry!" I heard below me, and looked down just as we barreled over the slack-jawed students. I tucked my knees up and was rewarded, if that's the right word, with the sight of one toppling backward over the other, hands still clutching his champagne bottle.

CHAPTER SIX

Whose Geas?

Before I had time to do more than gawk stupidly down at the vanishing Thames, we'd flashed through another cloud bank. The usual lurch, more tail-feathers floating on the wind as we emerged. You could feel right away something had changed; the medieval spires were gone and instead all around us were brick buildings, smokestacks, and (I flinched at a loud whistle) steamships. Mead gave a panicky flap or two, we dodged a barge, and Ed shouted triumphantly, "London!"

Mead, busy finding a flat roof, took a minute to reply. When we were finally settled atop a looming red-brick building whose rooftop was almost covered by sooty chimney pots, he released his grip on my shoulders with a long, slow groan that scared me a lot more than any of his earlier grumbling had.

"Mead?" I said, trying to keep my voice steadier than I felt.

"It's your claw, isn't it?" Ed sounded very like Granny as he stuck his hand out firmly. "Let me have a look."

To my surprise Mead held his right claw up without comment. Seeing it bent backward in a way no claw was ever meant to go, I couldn't help gasping a little, though I could have kicked myself right afterward. Neither Mead nor Ed spoke.

"Does it hurt too much for you to fly?" Ed asked after a long pause. Mead gazed away into the air as if he hadn't heard the question.

Finally, he did speak. "I can fly." We waited a minute, but that seemed to be his last word.

"I suppose," Ed said finally, "we'd better leave it as it is." The claw was twisted all the way around in a way that made me wince to look; turned upside down, almost.

"And I suppose," said Mead in a business-like way, turning to face me, "that we'd better think about what's next on our list, after the dun rose."

I could feel my heart pounding heavily against my ribs. Mead, injury or no injury, had managed our first two objects without a fuss. I was young and healthy (*Girl of the Ledge,* I found myself thinking with an even deeper sense of shame) but I'd failed utterly.

For some reason, Ed chose that moment to break into a series of choked little whinnies. He was laughing at me! And Mead gave what might have been a bird snicker. I forgot all about Mead's claw for a minute. I said hotly, "I tried my best, and I don't think it's nice to taunt me. Is it my fault it rolled away?"

My eyes were burning, but I willed myself not to let tears fall. Then Ed leaned forward and poked me in the ribs in the same way Ned had poked Morris. "Have you noticed what's in your right hand, Jen?"

Actually I hadn't given a thought to Morris's gift back on the ledge, the one I'd ignored because I was so busy thinking of what to say to him. I looked down. There, tucked tight into fingers that had turned white from gripping too hard, was the dun rose. Somehow, through all that dunking and spluttering, with "third time, third time" echoing in my ears, I'd never let it go.

As I tucked the rose into my bag, I asked, with transparently fake casualness, "Hey, what's a geas?" I tried to copy the old-fashioned sound of the word as Morris had said it.

Ed piped up right away. "Oh, I know that one! A geas is a holy order in Celtic myth. Like, umm, well you know how Cuchulainn couldn't refuse food from a woman? That was a geas."

"I didn't know that, actually, Ed, but thanks." I asked my next question of the open air. "Sooooo, any idea how that might relate to us?"

Ed stared at me blankly, then down to his notebook. That was fine; it wasn't his answer I wanted to hear.

"You might find," Mead began after a long pause, staring hard

at me, "that the word means something like the duty to keep working toward a certain goal. An office, they called it back when I was
young; later, I also heard it called a quest."

Mead's yellow eyes got brighter and more unblinking every time I
looked. Still, I stared right back, willing him to go on, not even letting myself get sidetracked into asking him when exactly he had ever
been young. Ever since I'd told him that Morris might need something, too, I'd had the feeling Mead was trying to prove something
to me. But what?

"And Morris," I said very slowly, "could tell I had a *geas* on me
because . . ." I trailed off, letting the silence between us deepen. I
could hear Ed nervously gnawing his pencil. Behind that, distant
sounds of London: horses, trains, a woman's voice—"Grapes, lovely
fresh grapes for sale!"

"The artist's *geas*," Mead finally said, "is a quest that rarely has
a very clear ending. It might seem to end with a particular artwork.
Yet the artist might find that once the single work was done, the feeling of obligation came back. The artist might even discover that the
desire to go on making was so strong even—" He stopped suddenly.

I looked up at once. "Even what, Mead?" I needed to know. His
head, though, was down among his wing-feathers now, carefully
smoothing out what few remained along his right wing tip. Very few.

He looked up. "If the geas were strong enough, even the artist's
death might only pass the quest onward, to a fellow artist, or a child,
or"—it was his turn to look up into the air at nobody in particular—
"to anyone at all."

"And that kind of passing . . . ," I said carefully, looking at Mead to see if he'd finish the sentence for me. Seeing his face remain blank, I drew a long breath and went on, ". . . might happen anytime. Is that right, Mead? The *geas* might suddenly burst back to life long after the artist died. Morris's *geas* might turn out to belong to Granny, or to somebody who read one of his books and got inspired, or to some kid who . . ."

In the pause that followed, the long silence in which nobody filled in my blank for me, in which only the scratch of Ed's pencil was audible, a new thought struck me. "You're no roc, Mead!" I announced.

"Thanks very much," he said promptly, in an aggrieved tone. "Did I ever say I was?"

"No, no," I exclaimed hastily, "of course not! But Morris did, back there"—I pointed back over my shoulder. "As if you were just some hideous animal schlepping me around. Anyway, you're not one!"

"Thanks again!" said Mead briskly. "Now, are we quite finished with this glorious festival of repetition?"

I wasn't quite done, though. "Because, Mead, what you actually are is a griffin!"

Ed gave a great shout of laughter, while Mead's feathers shot up in all directions. "I mean," I went on cheerily, "that you're half horse and half fierce bird of prey, like the one that threatens to eat a minor canon in that Maurice Sendak book." When I said the word "fierce," Mead's feathers started to settle a bit. After a minute, he gave a smug little cluck back in his throat (don't ask me how a cluck can sound smug, it just did). Then he gestured with his left wing toward an ominous staircase that led off the roof.

"It's October 1856, and we're perched above the London offices of the distinguished Gothic Revival architect Edmund Street. No crackers for guessing who his newest pupil might be. That doorway to your right leads down to Morris's third-floor office. He shares with a young man you should be careful not to underestimate. I'll be right here when you get back, and I expect you'll have with you . . . ?"

"A ship with shields before the sun," we both chorused obediently. Mead gave a very Napoleon-like *off you go* wave with his good claw. Off we went.

At the bottom of the dark moldy staircase we found ourselves right outside a door that, fortunately for us, had been recently oiled. It slid open noiselessly to reveal a beard glowing outrageously red in a shaft of sunlight: Morris, without a doubt. He was gabbling away excitedly at a young man bent over an architect's drafting table.

"Dear Webb," he was saying, "will I ever be as skilled an architect as you? No, no, don't bother to answer . . ." The young man looked sweet, a bit shy, almost exactly Morris's age. Morris rushed on.

"The fact is, Webb, the best work of all is to create a Gothic house. A book comes next, but never mind, I'll get to that in time, Webb, in due time."

Webb nodded agreeably and tossed in a "Quite right, Topsy,"; he was evidently listening only enough to keep Morris talking. It struck me that Morris was kind of an iPod for his friends. They liked to hear him talk while they worked in just about the same way I like listening to Regina Spektor when I'm practicing free throws.

"I'm no fool," Morris went on, "I know well enough that at the moment I'm just a young bungler tolerated because my father's grown rich in the stock market. But Philip, you are an architectural genius. Mind you, that's not to say anything against your, your, hmm, interior designs."

"Do you mean those little drinking glasses I've been working on, Topsy? With the green spirals?" the young man, who must have been Philip Webb, replied in a high, amiable voice, still not looking up from his careful drawing.

"Yes, yes, but not just those! Also the tables, and those marvelous painted cabinets you and Ned have started working on, and even your curious little Viking ship" (I felt Ed give a start behind me). "Yes, we'll call them all interior designs when we form our company."

"Company?" said Webb, looking up. "But aren't we here to be pupils, to learn to be architects and then . . . ?" He seemed not quite sure what to say next, as if he didn't know how the story turned out, but was counting on someone to tell him when the time came. I could sympathize.

Morris, though, slapped the table and laughed. "Our business, Webb, is to come together to make things of beauty, paying no mind to what the bankers and bishops say they want."

Webb gave a little chuckle—to me it seemed encouraging, companionable. For some reason, though, Morris erupted. He gave a furious grunt and stamped the floor, hard (Rumpelstiltskin, Rumpelstiltskin!). "Chuckle away, Webb, but a company to sell furniture, by God, can be a sacred trust, too! As sacred as anything accomplished by King Arthur's company of knights, with their—"

He spluttered, as close to a loss for words as I'd seen him, then regained speed. "—their maces and lances and unnamed hordes of servants to trail behind and mop away the blood."

"And what if our modern knights of Industry, with their blood-mopping servants, don't want to buy what you make, Topsy?" Webb asked mischievously.

"Ship," muttered Ed impatiently behind me. "Ship ship, where are you, ship?" Like him, I'd been scanning the room as Morris talked, but I still gave him an indignant elbow. Everything Morris said was telling me a little more about the *geas* that he was under. Or wait, was it me under the *geas*? I shook my head, trying to clear it.

"We'll make them want it, Webb," roared Morris, interrupting my train of thought by bounding in the air so indignantly and so vigorously that the floor trembled when he landed. *Rumpelstiltskin! Rumpelstiltskin!* "By heavens, I know enough to form a brother-hood that will make not only the best houses, but also the best win-dows, the best glasses, the best tiles—anything that would make the difference between misery and joy."

Webb was laughing, and looking at him with an expression I was beginning to recognize in Topsy's friends: It held amusement, admiration, and underneath something like the look Granny shot Ed and me when she thought we weren't watching. And just like that, Morris laughed, pulled out a huge sea-green handkerchief to wipe his brow, and the rage was over.

Ed leaned over to me. "You know what he reminds me of, when he goes off like that? Old Faithful!" Sixty seconds of steam and

fury, then placid as if it had never happened. Yeah, Ed was right. Topsy the geyser.

"We'll begin the business today, Webb. I have just the commis-sion." Morris was gabbling away cheerily, not a storm cloud in sight. Webb looked up inquiringly. "Build me a house," pronounced Mor-ris, stroking his growing beard importantly. "I shall be getting mar-ried soon and I imagine, yes, I *know* that we shall need a house.

"We'll need it because . . ." He looked puzzled for a minute: You could see him asking himself, *Why do people need houses?* Suddenly his face cleared. "Because"—Webb leaned forward eagerly—"I've got a staircase in mind that Ned and I saw in Rouen.

"I know I jotted it down." Morris was now looking around himself wildly. "On the inside cover of the Murray's guide to France . . ."

Just then Ed cleared his throat and shouted, in a weird echoey voice that made it sound as if he were far, far away, "Fire! Beware! Fire in the basement!" Philip and Morris glanced at each other and were gone in an instant, thundering past us (we hugged the wall as they whizzed by) and down the front stairs. I could hear William's bellow trailing away, "We'll call it Red House, Webb, Red House . . ."

The instant they'd gone by, Ed—grinning like a maniac—headed straight to a dusty little table across the room. He was back in seconds brandishing a gorgeous wooden model of a ship. Along its side, wink-ing as they caught gleams of sunlight streaming through the window, were a row of shields held aloft by tiny little wooden men.

CHAPTER SEVEN

The Return of the Roc

I couldn't tell you how we got out of there, but by the time Ed and I finished hugging each other and retelling the whole story, we were spiraling back over Oxford. Ed was busy pretending not to watch Mead's feathers fall, but when he muttered some numbers to me, I realized I hadn't been listening for some time now. My mind had been wandering back to our last hours at home, right before all of this—whatever *this* was—had happened. Something had really bothered me, and I finally figured it out. Ed was happy as a clam now. And why not? He was on the adventure he'd always dreamed of, one that needed lots of notebooks, plenty of facts about history, and a fair amount of calculating. Back before we had hit the Tapestry, though, while we were hearing Mr. Nazhar's letter, he'd been devastated, just as

sad as Granny. So why had at least a part of me been happy when we heard the news?

Slumping forward against Mead's warm back, I went back to that moment again and I was sure of it. Even though most of my mind was thinking about Granny and how sad she must be feeling and how Ed would really, really, really hate having to move, some tiny part of me (the attic-window part, I guess, that looks down on my life as if it's a totally different realm) had been happily shouting "I'm free!" I could reconstruct the exact train of thought. Who cared if we could trace the Tapestry back to William Morris or not? Imaginary is imaginary. If we couldn't sell the Tapestry, that was the final proof that we'd been living inside some kind of fantasy all this time. We'd have to rejoin the real, everyday world.

As our slow downward spiral continued, I asked myself why I'd been so furious lately, even mad at my own parents when I looked at their pictures taped to the edge of my bedroom mirror. I knew it had something to do with Granny's teaching tailing off, and with Mr. Nazhar being more or less the only visitor we could count on. Sometimes I hate that it's my job to be the family memory. Ed got all the good stuff from my parents: He bends his head low over his notebook like a cat drinking from a stream and I can see Mom. Me, all I got was a bunch of useless images, like snapshots—Mom and Dad climbing onto their old bikes, or wandering along a frozen river, both talking a mile a minute.

Of course, I wanted to believe it when Granny said that as long as we kept making art and thinking about it, we were still connected to Mom and Dad. But I couldn't imagine trying to explain it even to Eva, who I hoped was still sort of my best friend, let alone to our star forward Sally, who might be Eva's best friend now. So when I turned fourteen back in April, I made a resolution to stop listening when Granny talked about "weaving you into their warp"—and I'd pretty much decided that the arts high school downtown was out, that I'd stick with Eva and the team.

Suddenly I had a vision: a picture lit up for me, like a close-up in a movie. Eva was running down the street in her field hockey gear, heading for the high school practice field with Sally and Grace. I could feel my legs flexing to run after her, freed at last from the weight of the Tapestry.

I groaned: How pathetic could I be? Was I really wasting my time getting jealous of Eva's new sport, and her new friends? I couldn't stand field hockey! Something Eva had told me the day before we got the letter came back to me: "If you could stop talking about your granny when I'm trying to tell you about boys, Jen, I think you might have a better chance." *At what?* I'd been too ashamed to ask her then, but all of a sudden I had really wanted to know.

"That's it, I'm through!" I said aloud. This was why the museum's letter had sent a little thrill through me. If I didn't have the Tapestry around to dream about, then what I'd mostly be would be Eva's friend, and a good athlete, and, and, well I didn't know what exactly, but a lot of things that Ed and Granny knew nothing about.

◆　　　◆　　　◆

Just then I felt a jolt, and a rush of air next to me, as if someone had opened the door between subway cars. Instinctively I gripped my knees around Mead, and everything that had just happened came flooding back to me.

I groaned. As usual, my timing was perfect: When Eva wanted to talk about high school I was too busy thinking about William Morris. But now that I was ready to give up on that art school, and start being who Eva wanted me to be, here I was trapped in Tapestry land.

"Through with what?" asked Ed curiously, looking back over his shoulder.

"Oh, never mind, Ed, for Pete's sake!" I snapped, exasperated at myself, and he retreated quickly to his notebook. I sighed. As we touched down on a steep-roofed building, just outside an enormous rose window, I touched his arm. "Oh, Ed, I'm just mad at myself. It's . . ." But he'd stopped listening. I couldn't really blame him; I didn't feel much like listening to me, either.

Where were we? It was clearly not a church, but it was just as massive. Possibly a library: I caught a glimpse of rows and rows of books down below through its open rose windows. Involuntarily, my nose wrinkled. *Yeeeeerrgh;* what was that smell?

Mead coughed discreetly, wiped his wing over his nose. "Linseed oil, turpentine, and rabbit-skin glue," he explained. "Morris and the Pre-Raphaelites are painting a mural here." He sniffed long and disapprovingly. "The proportions, though, are certainly off. Fading, I distinctly foresee fading."

I decided I would have lived in fear with Mead as a teacher. On a sudden impulse I asked him, "Mead, did you once live with Morris?"

Mead shot me the same glance that Morris had thrown at Ned when he met the Pre-Raphaelites. He slowly opened his mouth to answer.

But just then Ed gave me an urgent poke. "Okay, Jen, listen to the next one:

> "A man drew near
> With painted shield and gold-wrought spear.
> Good was his horse and grand his gear."

"Be quiet, Ed!" I barked; I really needed to know what Mead was about to say. But it was too late. Mead turned his head away, cleared his throat massively (a faint odor of granola bar wafted over me), and nodded. "Jen," he said gravely, "your brother is right. The poem brought us to the great hall of the Oxford Union debating society for a reason."

So it was the poem doing this? Nothing made sense to me.

Right now, though, as I struggled to clamber off Mead's back and onto the narrow window ledge (trying not to look down at the grim stone pavement below), I had a more pressing problem. "Mead!" I hissed urgently. "If the poem wants us to grab a figure from the mural, how am I supposed to fit that into my gym bag?"

Mead looked back impassively at me, which I guess meant *figure it out*. That wasn't going to be so easy. Even with all the rearranging I could manage, the ship barely fit. Of all the random memories, I suddenly found myself thinking back to the end of *The Hobbit*, when Bilbo is trying to figure out how he could possibly bring even one-fourteenth of the dragon's treasure back home with him to the Shire. If Ed and I survived this and came home, I thought, I'd quit making fun of Bilbo, or his pony, or his chests of silver and of gold.

Did that also mean I'd have more sympathy for Ed when he agonized about fitting all his survival gear into our backpack for a weekend hike? Nope. It felt a lot easier to sympathize with Bilbo than Ed. Still, I grinned down at him fondly. "Painted shield, spear, good horse; check."

Suddenly, from far below us, I could hear a familiar voice bellowing instructions. The words faded in and out: "Careful preparations . . . suitable cooling period . . . tempering the plaster to prevent fading."

Then I gave a frightened shudder. Right around the corner from us, a good forty feet off the ground, someone yelled back: "Oh, yes, Topsy, temper, temper, temper!" with a suave, devil-may-care laugh.

I was sure I recognized the know-it-all voice. "Rossetti!" said Ed accusingly. Instead of ssshing him, Mead nodded gravely, looking suddenly a little older. I risked a sneaky glance down his side, looking for more missing feathers.

Moments later I heard delicate silvery laughter from down below. Two female voices echoed Rossetti's pun delightedly, "Oh yes Mr. Morris, temper, temper, hahahahahaha!"

I gave a start. If there was one thing that had been missing since we'd landed on Mead's back, it was certainly women. Was there a Pre-Raphaelite Sisterhood of artists we didn't know about? Ed gave Mead the *there's something you're not telling us* look. But Mead, without seeming to cower or look guilty, had a trick of refusing to meet our eyes when he didn't feel like talking. He pulled it now.

With as little noise as we could manage, we slid ourselves inside the nearest rose window, tucked behind a wooden post. From here, we could see Rossetti, no more than five feet away, dangling like Peter Pan from a rope harness while dabbing furiously away at the mural.

There was a significant pause: Was Mead going to tell us anything about the laughter down below? Finally he cleared his throat almost inaudibly. "Ah, yes, children," he whispered. "It seems we've arrived at a very delicate time for William Morris and Dante Gabriel"— if birds had had lips instead of beaks, I think Mead's would have curled slightly—"Rossetti." Was Mead embarrassed about something? He went on, "You see, both William and Gabriel have been lucky enough to meet the women of their dreams. If you crane your heads and catch sight of that slender girl down there, yes, sipping out of the blue bottle, that's Lizzie Siddal. She was Gabriel's muse, his model, his pupil, and, eventually, his wife."

I stole a glance down. She seemed oddly familiar: I heard Ed flipping through his notebook furiously and then he whispered. "She's that drowned girl Millais painted, right? Ophelia."

Mead nodded. "Yes, quite right Edward, the brotherhood shared their techniques very freely—and their models as well."

I found it hard to listen to them, because I couldn't take my eyes off the other woman. I'd seen so her face so often in Granny's books that she swam up at me like a dream, or someone I'd known all my life. I'd seen her painted waking and sleeping, thoughtful and sad, young and old. But I'd never before seen her laughing and happy. Another odd memory flooded over me: I was on my mother's lap looking at patterns. Her arms were around me, guiding my finger from one embroidery to another. My fingers would pick out one face on every page. The same face, over and over.

"And that," I said, pointing, "is Jane Burden, the eighteen-year-old daughter of a groom. She lives in miserable St. Helen's Passage." For some reason I found my neck getting warm. "When she's lucky she and her sister Bessie get work sewing. And she's beautiful beautiful beautiful." Ed was staring at me bug-eyed, the way he did when I picked a fight.

Jane, with her pale skin and red hair, that long face and dark sad eyes, tugged at me in some familiar way. I could almost feel a comforting set of arms close around me as I gazed down at her. I put out a finger as if I could trace her face on a page—then hastily I made the finger instead point down toward where Jane stood nervously twining a strand of Lizzie's hair in her hand. I hurried on: "She's the model for all the Pre-Raphaelites, but it's William Morris who's going to write on the back of his painting of her, I CAN'T PAINT YOU, BUT I LOVE YOU. And he's the one she's going to marry."

For a minute we all took the scene in: Morris was busy watch-ing Jane, who in turn was busy watching Rossetti as he dangled by the mural, his lips twisted in thought and his brush in constant motion.

The murals were growing all around us, and I had a thought. "That's Lancelot, looking for the Holy Grail," I whispered, looking at the sleeping figure painted right below us. "But there's something not quite right about the story, isn't there, Mead? Something that stands in Lancelot's way?"

"Someone," Mead corrected gently, and tilted his head toward the figure, tall, beautiful, and clad all in green, that Rossetti was work-ing on now. With those swollen lips and the sad eyes I knew so well from Granny's books, that could only be Jane in the mural. So if Morris was about to marry her, how could Rossetti be spending all his time painting this picture of Jane? Jane looking down sadly, and longingly, at a beautiful tall knight who resembled—I couldn't help thinking—Rossetti himself.

"Mead?" I said, forgetting our *geas* in my confusion about how these artists and their models all fit together. "Why is Rossetti draw-ing that picture of Jane . . . ?"

"That's Guinevere," said Mead firmly. "He's painting Guinev-ere, the wife of Arthur, his king and his closest friend." I nodded, but I still wasn't sure I understood it all completely.

"Well, why was Rossetti so interested in the story of Guinevere's love for Lancelot instead of her husband, Arthur?" I asked. I felt the same kind of itch I always did reading Sherlock Holmes stories.

There was a vital fact missing, and until I had it, I couldn't figure out the villain—or even what the crime had been in the first place.

I felt suddenly exasperated. "How do artists ever pick their sub-ject matter, anyway? In class, you always know if it's an apple or a face you're supposed to be working on. But for Rossetti—"

"In fact," Mead cut in suddenly, "Morris grew interested in that story, too. While Rossetti was painting Jane as Guinevere, Morris had begun writing poems. Both told the same story. It was Guine-vere's love for her husband's friend Lancelot that finally destroyed the Round Table. And perhaps"—here Mead gave me a look that I recognized well from Granny, though I couldn't quite say what it meant—"*that* is why Guinevere in Rossetti's paintings is looking so very sad."

Art was a funny thing. I had always assumed that artists painted the world the way they wanted it to be—that was what beauty meant, wasn't it? Yet sometimes they couldn't help making art instead that showed the thing they most feared. What must it have meant to Morris to paint Jane as Guinevere if he thought that he was doomed to play Arthur while Rossetti got to be Lancelot? And what about Rossetti? Did he think of himself as the noble, beautiful Lancelot, longing for Guinevere?

How was Guinevere was supposed to choose between Arthur and Sir Lancelot anyway? I don't know how long I'd been turning this over in my mind, trying to work up the courage to ask Mead, when suddenly I heard Rossetti gave an outraged shout.

"Ridiculous urchin! Give that drawing back this instant!" Ed,

shaking with fear, but with sparkling eyes, scrambled up behind Mead desperately trying to tuck something into my bag. Even with the panic surging through me, I couldn't help admiring Rossetti's delicate pencil sketch of a mounted knight with shield and spear.

As Mead tore into the sky, though, I stopped thinking about Guinevere and Camelot. I heard the *rrrrip* of little metal teeth unhooking. The zipper on my gym bag!

Before our whole quest fell on Jane Burden's head, I reached my left hand around desperately, trying to pull the unzipped sides together enough to hold in the apple (I felt it rolling under my left hand) and the pilgrim shell (my right thumb had it pinned against the nylon). As I scrabbled to pull the zipper tight, I felt my basket-ball roll, teeter, and slip out of my bag. If the paint bucket was where I think it was, I may have hit the first three-point shot in English history.

As the clouds closed on us again, I could just make out Morris's delighted yelp: "Ahhhhh, the return of the roc!"

Chapter Eight

Art for a few

 " **h** ey, Mead, how do you use the clouds to move us through time?" Ed was asking earnestly as we pulled out of our next dive. His pencil was poised, as if he expected Mead to start reciting the formulas right away. A quick wing and a beady glare was all he got before Mead settled on slippery red tiles. Below us was a steeply pitched roof, and then beneath that apple trees and green lawns spreading out on every side.

"London's second Great International Exhibition is about to open. It's spring of 1862, and Morris did build a house for himself, after all," Mead said briskly, sliding open a trapdoor and ushering us into the crawl space at the top of an amazing open stairwell.

We gasped. The ceiling and walls were covered with heavy, twisting curved figures of blue and green paint. I caught my breath; it felt like being inside an abstract painting. "Could those be rows of paramecia?" whispered Ed excitedly, hanging with his head upside down to gawk. (I hate it when he talks about paramecia.) Suddenly there were footsteps in the hall, and Mead hooked Ed back out of sight with a neat sweep of the claw.

"Well, Topsy? It's been two years. What do you think of your Red House after all?" A young man I instantly recognized as Webb came into view, his arms full of beautiful, delicate glasses and plates.

"Webb, it's the beautifullest place on Ea . . . aaaaawwwgh! That's my beard, my beard, my *beard!*" Close behind Webb, Morris's arms were also full, but with a different burden. A baby and a toddler both laughed delightedly as he spun around and around like a drunk bear, trying to disentangle his wayward beard from the hands of his . . . daughters? I turned back to Mead for confirmation. How a bird without eyelashes, lips, or cheeks can look down on someone dotingly I can't really say; but he did it. As Mead continued to totter forward with the happily shrieking children, Ed found the relevant facts in his notebook.

"Jenny and May Morris, born January 1861 and March 1862; children of William and . . ." Remembering my outburst back at the Oxford Union, Ed politely paused to let me finish.

"Jane Burden Morris," I finished smoothly. "And," I added with a grin, studying Ed's face, "Perhaps you'd like to guess the name of the young mother who got up on rickety ladders to stencil those paramecia?"

By this time, Jane had disentangled little Jenny and May from Morris, tumbling down to the ground and tickling them into whoops of laughter. Morris flopped down panting beside Webb and Burne-Jones, on a bench that had been painted with oaks, river meadows, and dappled woodland.

"Right, Ned," Morris said busily, "this exhibition is going to make or mar us. Customers need to be sure that we shall always have something truly new to give them."

Ned nodded. "They should feel that if they want to they can live inside an interior designed by Morris, Marshall, Faulkner, and Company."

"Yes!" burst in Morris explosively. "That's exactly the point. An interior! Not just isolated works." Everyone nodded cheerfully.

Their smiles faded, though, as he went on. "Besides the stained glass, carving, metalwork, chintzes, and carpets, what have we really got?"

Ned and Webb looked stunned. "Well, Topsy; be reasonable! The firm is only a year old," Ned finally ventured. "Isn't that plenty?"

"Nonsense!" said Morris severely, bustling off down a long low corridor while Ned and Philip followed obediently ("Make way for ducklings," I whispered to Ed). "We can do much better than that. Let's have a look upstairs in the workshop."

Ed and I froze stock-still on the ceiling, inadequately sheltered by a couple of roof-beams, as the procession trooped upstairs and along a long hallway to Morris's study. He made such a fuss and bustle getting settled in that we were able to relocate to a sheltered alcove just outside the door. "Perfect for snatch and bolt," Ed muttered as we settled in.

"Here we are!" Morris was at his desk tossing papers from side to side with abandon. I could still hear the girls giggling downstairs; behind that, though, I thought I heard some heavy footsteps and—could that be a man's laugh?

"No, no," Morris was saying with rising irritation, "that's the sketches for my *Aeneid*. Hmm, that's a birthday manuscript for your wife Georgiana, Ned, don't look! I'm not happy with the tempera for that one, too yolky . . . Hmm, saga translation, no . . . ink tests, no . . . grrrr—" It suddenly occurred to me that Morris was only a few seconds away from another one of those geyser eruptions.

Instead, he gave a delighted cry. His whole face changed as he held up an exquisitely worked drawing of small brightly colored birds—woodpeckers, I guessed, darting toward a snarled tendril of roses that clung tightly around a wooden frame.

And those petals; those petals. Ed began to whisper to me, but I knew what he was about to say. Smiling back over my shoulder, I mouthed the line along with him: "Through the cold garden boughs we went / Where the tumbling roses shed their scent."

"It's from that central Red House courtyard, you know, right by that porch I call Pilgrim's Rest." Morris gazed down at the drawing more or less the same way he'd been looking at his two daughters grabbing at his beard.

"Yes, Topsy, it certainly makes Red House come alive," Ned said finally. "But what exactly . . . ?"

Morris crowed in delight. "Wallpaper, of course!"

He laughed again at their dumbfounded faces. "Of course I know that finding a way to print onto the right kind of paper won't be easy—I was thinking that some of the printers these days are experi-menting with zinc plates."

As the shocked silence persisted, he gave another easy laugh. "Don't gape at me like that! I admit they'll be hard to master, but surely we can have something ready for the Exhibition."

Looking around at their skeptical faces, waiting for belief to blossom, he grunted and made a slight concession. "Fine, fine! Say it takes us eighteen months, perhaps as long as two years." ("Ah, a rare moment of candor in forecasting by Mr. Morris!" Mead whispered drily in my ear.) "That's a crimp in production, I admit, but think of how easy it will be to distribute once we get all the colors right! Imagine if every customer . . ."

I jumped suddenly as I heard from the corridor behind me that same easy laugh I'd heard a moment ago. That Rossetti had a habit of sneaking up on you.

"Well, well," he said, striding smoothly by us into the room. Morris and the others went oddly still as he spoke. "Look at that marvelous drawing! I told you Red House was a wonder of the age, but this, this, well, it's quite perfect."

Rossetti plucked the wallpaper drawing from Morris's hands, and curled and uncurled it idly as he spoke. "I must protest, though, gentle Topsy, against your plans. Imagine gluing some-thing as beautiful as this on just *any*body's wall. Surely you don't think that every passerby with a few half crowns to rub against one another can walk away from our showroom with a sheet of your design crumpled up in his, his . . ."

A chill was in the air. Ned and Webb were both looking out the

window with great concentration. Morris's face had turned red as I'd ever seen it—redder even than when we'd seen him charging his pony against imaginary enemies as a little boy. "In his dirty hands, Gabriel? Is that it? Well, if those hands are dirty from ink, from London grime, from the workshops, they're no dirtier than the hands that made the drawing in the first place. If I can get this process right I'll sell the paper for a shilling, or sixpence."

A pause while Morris fumed and reddened and everybody else paled—except Rossetti, whose face was already plenty white, and whose hands shook no more now than they had when he'd first walked in. "By God!" Morris bellowed finally, "I'd be delighted to sell it for tuppence a roll, if I thought people would buy it. I'd like it in every filthy kitchen in Pimlico, on every crumbling Cheapside wall."

Uh-oh. I crouched down and braced myself as Morris's voice boomed out, "I'd happily share a stage with you if you'd care to talk about art and its uses to the stinking masses, or the perfumed ones. But when it comes to deciding who truly *deserves*"—he rolled the word through his lips like a curse—"to be exposed to art, I have little to say. I long ago left off telling people what they were or were not worthy to possess." He took a deep breath. "Even you, dear, dear friend. Even you."

There was a pause, during which Rossetti involuntarily stepped backward, not speaking but never taking his eyes from Morris's face. With a pang, I suddenly remembered my dad prowling up and down the same way Morris was now—a leopard caged behind bars that only he could see. And I saw Arthur in Camelot, looking across the Round Table at a Lancelot he knows will betray him.

Rossetti was staring at the blank wall opposite as if some fascinating thing of beauty hung there. "If I won't stand in the way of those I love when they do what I hate," Morris went on heavily. "Can you really expect I'll prevent those I barely know from taking my pictures home for any reason they please? They can outfit their favorite dachshund in this Trellis wallpaper; and by God I'll thank them for it as they walk out the door!"

Morris quivered to a halt, breathing hard through his nose.

"Goodness," said Rossetti, looking down, "I see how much you've been affected by the loss of your father's fortune." I don't know how he did it, but Rossetti somehow made "father" sound like a dirty word. Ned and Philip both took in slight hissing breaths—nobody looked at Morris, and nobody moved. "Yes," Rossetti went on absently, running his hand up and down the drawing, "*such* a pity about those copper stocks, Topsy, really, who would have thought they could just vanish?

"Still," he went on cheerily, ignoring the solemn faces turned toward him, "the realm, thank goodness, remains filled with wealthy patrons. I should hope there's no real need for you, for *us,* to descend from the arts proper to the, the, the . . ."

"Lesser arts?" suggested Morris in a voice that was a good deal steadier than his flaming skin and drumming fingers would have suggested. There was a long pause, and then Webb moved forward gently, taking the Trellis drawing from Morris's hand and tucking it precariously away in a side pocket.

Ned said quietly, like someone reciting a poem or a prayer, "I do not want art for a few . . ."

As he trailed off, Morris, barely moving his lips, finished the sentence: ". . . any more than education for a few, or freedom for a few." The two looked at one another briefly, then away.

Another long pause—I could hear Ed and Mead breathing beside me, and nothing else. "Right," said Webb after a long pause. "I suppose I'll get started with those zinc plates."

If Burne-Jones and Morris had just scored against Rossetti, he was doing his best not to show it. He yawned elaborately and stood up. "Well, Topsy and *Company*"—I don't think I imagined the sneer on this word, either—"I have got to see a lord, a very wealthy lord more's the pleasure, about a commission. A Blessed Damozel for his mantelpiece."

He tilted his head so his hair cascaded perfectly off the shoulders of his tattered smock. Annoying as I found him at this particular moment, I still couldn't help admiring his paint-specked artist's clothes, and the blistered hands that registered every trace of his long hours at the easel.

"Well," he went on absently, gazing down at a seam that had begun to fray, "I'll stop by next week to, as Keats would have said, '*cash up*' my share in the business. Though what business the poet had talking about cash, whether up or down, I'm sure I cannot rightly imagine!" With a faint, satisfied chuckle, Rossetti drifted away. Webb was so absorbed in gazing after him that he didn't notice Ed's hand stealthily extracting the drawing of "Where the tumbling roses shed their scent" from that conveniently gaping pocket.

CHAPTER NINE

Goliath's Head

Ed and I were quiet as Mead pushed us high above London, west along the Thames under a leaden sky. I tried to ignore the hole that had opened up in the feathers along Mead's neck, and the occasional lurch or jolt as he struggled to stay straight. It struck me suddenly that while Morris was as chubby-cheeked and happy as ever, Mead was showing the years. Somehow a price was being paid for every jump we made—and it wasn't hard to guess who was paying it.

How long could Mead hold out with us on his back? And if he couldn't? If the next time we went to take off he simply couldn't manage it, what then? I unwrapped a granola bar from my bag (only two more) and slipped it down to Mead. I caught a gleam of a smile in his eye as he snapped it neatly into his beak—but only a gleam.

"Ed." I tried for a low, calm voice. "Can we go through the poem again, try to see where we stand?" Without a word he handed me the notebook, already turned to the right page.

I started by reading the first part of the poem out loud, reassuring myself about what we'd already managed to do:

> I am the ancient Apple-Queen,
>
> For evermore a hope unseen,
>
> Betwixt the blossom and the bough.

"That one was easy!" I said as chirpily as I could manage.

"Child's play," agreed Mead between bites, pausing to wipe a sticky bit of oat off one side of his face.

> A gourd and a pilgrim shell, roses dun,
>
> A ship with shields before the sun.

"Well," said Mead immediately, "the pilgrim will be fine, I'm sure of it. And as for the dun rose—"

"The dun rose," broke in Ed unexpectedly, "was just plain awe-some!"

"The ship was routine," I said, finding myself getting into the spirit now; it felt like a scavenger hunt.

"And so was:

"A man drew near,
With painted shield and gold-wrought spear.
Good was his horse and grand his gear."

"And you, Edward," cut in Mead, "proved yourself well suited to burgling when it came to:

"Through the cold garden boughs we went
Where the tumbling roses shed their scent."

I checked my gym bag to confirm the inventory. "Apple, shell and gourd, dun rose, ship with shields, pencil sketch of knight on horseback, cold garden boughs on wallpaper," I recited quickly.

"Okay," I went on, trying to ignore the rumbling in my stomach and the longing for home that came with it. *Don't think about it,* I told myself sternly, shoving away Granny's face when it popped into view. "So, here's what's left.

"Therefore Venus well may we
Praise the green ridges of the sea.
A fork-tongued dragon fresh and fell
Behold I have loved faithfully and well.
Beside dark hills whose heath-bloom feeds no bee,
All birds sing in the town of the tree.
In the white-flowered hawthorn brake
Love be merry for my sake.

And Thames runs chill
'Twixt mead and hill."

"It's getting trickier now," said Ed, in his best chess-player voice. I shot a questioning glance back over my shoulder at him.

"The ones we've had so far," he went on, "all turned out to be objects, which made them easy. And I guess the dragon could be that straightforward—"

"And the birds that 'sing in the town of the tree,' too," I jumped in.

Ed gave an exasperated snort that made Mead shoot us a quick worried glance. "But where's Venus and the green ridges of the sea?" Ed's flat pessimistic tone was starting to worry me. "Or Love being merry for my sake? And how are we supposed to collect the Thames running chill?"

I had no answers for Ed's questions—and to judge from his silence, Mead didn't, either. If he was even listening to us anymore.

At that moment the poem seemed like only half my troubles any-way. When Morris had tucked that rose in my hand and talked about my *geas*, he'd triggered a set of thoughts it was hard for me to control, or even make sense of. Now, with a warm southern wind lifting Mead above the clouds into a sunny zone, I found myself starting to doze as we flew. As my head dipped and my eyes flickered (open, closed, open again), a thought popped into my head: *Well, what then if happiness is gone? How do I make my art from woe?*

And just like that (I was probably doomed not to sleep in the entire nineteenth century, I thought bitterly) I was awake again.

How had that thought crept into me? I looked back through my memories, trying to figure out where that *woe* had come from. The fight? Something Morris had said? Was it something in his eyes, maybe, in the way he'd sighed, or in what he hadn't said?

Dozing again, I began to feel my fingers tingling. The world split in two; half of me was still there clutching Ed's waist on Mead's back. But the other half of me was sitting in front of a zinc plate, painstakingly etching the lines of Trellis onto it. The chemicals you needed to do that kind of work—my nose wrinkled just thinking of them, the chlorides and manganates, and those corrosive acids to fix the design for good. I took a deep breath as I leaned over the plate, and found I could smell them, putrid as a rotting carcass. I put my hand to my nose and sneezed twice, hard.

"Uh, Jen?" Ed said in a dazed voice. Mead was craning his neck to stare at me with open concern.

"Gesundheit!" I said confusedly. "What's the matter?"

"Nothing's the matter now, Jen," said Ed, choosing his words carefully. "Only a minute ago you were acting like you couldn't even hear or see us; your head was down, your arms were kind of twitch-ing in front of you, like you were a . . ." He trailed off, looking for the right words to convey it. "Like a changeling!" he said finally.

I knew we were going there. Ed's secretly obsessed with the idea of fairies that change babies at birth, and sooner or later all his ideas come back to the possibility that somebody might have been *changed* without knowing it.

If I was changing now, though, it wasn't fairies that had done it.

All I'd been doing was thinking about Morris, and his life, when suddenly it was as if I could feel what he'd been doing. As if . . .

"Jen!" Mead's head had come all the way around over his shoulder (how did he do that?) and he'd tapped my leg hard with his beak. I jerked upright. "I need you here with me, Jen, not daydreaming about wallpaper, or sneezing like a rheumy camel!"

"But Mead," I said confusedly, "I think I can tell what Morris is feeling. He was at work, and I knew just what he was thinking, just what his hands wanted to do. That could help us somehow."

Mead clicked irritably. "Yes, Jen, yes you can know what he felt, and even what he thought as well. You can know it because . . ." Then evidently Mead thought better of it.

"Because why?" Ed asked eagerly, and if I hadn't been pretending to be too angry to listen, I'd have asked him also. Mead only tssked, though, and flapped heavily on, slowly pulling us back toward the few faintly visible cloud banks high above.

I kept tussling with that question while we descended into a leafy Thames-side London neighborhood. Mead was ignoring me. When I tugged on his shoulder, careful not to dislodge what feathers were still there, he cleared his throat and put on his best tour-guide voice. "Allow me to alert you young visitors to the many virtues of Kelmscott House, the suburban London retreat Morris and his family moved into when their business was really booming. Notice its lovely garden, the five huge windows for watching the traffic on the Thames, even the carriage house with plenty of space for industrial experiments." I could almost see shiny museum-guard brass buttons on his chest.

I tried to sound stern anyway. "Mead, I need to know what happened to me back then. And that means you have to tell me more about Morris and his family."

Mead gave no sign he'd heard me. Instead, he kept an eye on Ed's scribbling pencil and said, "All their printing and bookmaking and photographic friends lived nearby. The house was a center for everything exciting in the world of design. Stained glass, for instance."

By now we were crouched on a steaming basement windowsill. Industrial sounds—cutting, punching, shifting of heavy machinery—came from inside.

"Mead! Cut it out! We really need to talk about Morris and his woe."

"Their gorgeous stained glass," Mead went on doggedly, "was a revelation to American makers like Tiffany. Somehow they managed to combine storytelling with beautifully abstract designs, with patterns that came out of nature and yet crystallized in the furnace . . ."

I stamped my foot so hard, I almost lost my footing on the ledge. "Mead! I'm not talking about stained glass now!" Ed looked up from his notebook with the same vacant stare he gets when he's calculating batting averages.

I kept my eyes steadily fixed on Mead, who was now giving me his undivided attention. "What's going on? There's something I don't understand. Morris is making art and writing poetry by the bucketful—everybody loves it!"

I broke off, frustrated, tried to think about what grown-ups needed to be happy. I decided to be systematic. "I mean, okay, his work is good, right?" Mead nodded. "His wife is beautiful, right?" Mead looked at me sideways, as if that wasn't quite the right question. "Sad," I added, "she always looks sad, too." Mead nodded gravely. I filed that away. "Okay, so Jane is beautiful, but . . ." Jane still reminded me of someone, and I couldn't think who.

I shook my head and tried to focus. What else was I missing? "And his children? Mead? How about his children?"

For answer, Mead pointed his good left claw toward an open window. Inside, I could see a cheerfully manic girl, probably about twelve, with curly red hair that gave her an unmistakable mini-Morris look. She was busily grinding glass shards with a massive industrial-sized pestle and chattering away nonstop to Burne-Jones—his beard grayer and wispier, but otherwise unchanged.

"So, that's May?" Mead nodded. Then he swiveled his head toward a window to our left, which opened onto a different room. Craning my neck, I could see two adults kneeling by a bed. Morris and Jane. Over their crouched backs I could just make out a thrashing form, limbs moving and head tossing in a way that simply could not be right. My stomach gave a lurch. "Jenny?"

Mead didn't say anything for a minute. Then he said slowly, "Imagine discovering that your oldest child will fall down in fits for the rest of her life. That when the seizures come she can't speak, can't think straight, that her eyes roll back in her head—"

"Epilepsy," said Ed immediately, "grand mal epilepsy; right, Mead?"

"It's an easy diagnosis, perhaps, in an age when there's a pill for everything. For Morris, in an age of bloodletting and guesswork . . ." Mead clicked his beak sharply and looked away.

"Why?" It was Ed who spoke up now, twisting his hands nervously together as he watched Morris spread his arms over Jenny in the bed as if he could cover her like an umbrella. "It's not as if Morris gave her epilepsy. He loved her. He, he . . ."

Ed trailed off, but I jumped right in. "Don't you get it? He had those crazy fits his whole life, those red rages when he'd scream at anyone who came near him." I glared at Mead, even though I was pretty sure it wasn't him I was mad at right now. "So is that it, Mead? He blamed himself?"

Mead gave an impatient tssk. "Come along," he said abruptly, back in Mary Poppins mode—though he looked a lot scruffier than Mary Poppins ever did. "Come have a look at the stained glass Burne-Jones has just finished. It's for Trinity Church in Boston."

Ed obediently moved back to the window, looking down into the glass foundry. So quietly that only I could hear, Mead whispered, "Morris gets sick when Jenny does, simple as that. When times are good, he writes her silly letters, puts on a puppet play, spends all day cooking her an absurd feast. When the seizures don't leave off—" Mead paused. "—it's as if both of them are seized at once."

Meanwhile Ed was giggling, eyes glued to the window. Morris had just come into the room and was standing absolutely slack-jawed, staring. Meanwhile Ned, in front of the biggest stained-glass window I'd ever seen, was explaining something to Morris.

"You see, Topsy, it's King David giving his son Solomon final instructions about the building of the First Temple in Jerusalem. There are the beautiful attendant lords and ladies you designed, and over here on the right we see scenes from David's boyhood."

"And Daddy," May broke in with an exuberant wave of the arms I recognized at once as her father's own gesture. "What's more important in David's life than the moment he killed Goliath?"

There was a long pause while Morris took it all in. "So naturally," he said, "naturally you had to show David bearing Goliath's head back in triumph?"

"Oh yes," May said, with some of the same coolness of Ned. "And naturally for Goliath we needed to draw a very, very impressive head, didn't we?"

"So what you're saying," roared Morris, "is that you're actually paying me a *compliment* by decapitating me and sticking my head up there on the window?"

May giggled delightedly and clapped her hands. "See, Neddy, I just knew he'd understand." Then all three of them threw back their heads and laughed like banshees, Morris loudest of them all.

When the tears had come and gone, and everyone had pounded

everyone else's shoulders at least a dozen times—May only got knocked down once—Morris said, "Well, let's only hope they get the joke in Boston. It's a pity we won't be there to see it."

"Of course not. You'll be right here with us." Ned shot Morris a quick look. "Right here, isn't that so, Daddy?"

"Well, well, May, here's how it is," said Ned finally. "Your mother is taking you down to see your new house in Oxfordshire. Your uncle Gabriel will be there to look after things and keep you company. But your father has decided to accept an invitation from his friend Erik Magnusson to visit Iceland."

"Eiríkr," said Morris promptly.

"Yes of course, Eiríkr," Ned continued hastily; May was looking dumbfounded. "It's the land of the Viking sagas. And the dragons. And the volcanoes. And, the, ah, ah . . ." He gazed appealingly at Morris.

Morris, though, didn't see him—because he and May were staring at each other gleefully. Both of them shouted together, "The tölting Icelandic horses!"

With a huge smile, Morris pulled out of his pocket a furled piece of paper, tossed it over to May. "I've got a puzzle today that's too hard even for you, May, let alone Neddy. So I'll give you a hint: a goddess in verse."

With a practiced hand May uncurled the sheet and looked at him sharply—this was obviously a game they'd played many times. A rebus? A riddle? I glimpsed a female figure perched atop what from this distance looked like a wavy rectangle of green.

As May's eyes lit up in pleased recognition, I suddenly felt a switch go in my head. Again that feeling of being somehow connected (plugged in, maybe) came over me. Only this time it was May's place I took, her eyes I suddenly saw out of. I knew this one by heart!

I mouthed along with her:

Therefore Venus well may we
Praise the green ridges of the sea.

I turned away then, my head suddenly spinning. The moment had passed, and I still could make no sense of it. I turned to Mead for an explanation, but he held up a commanding claw for silence. May had turned to Morris and asked, with an impish grin, "Only Daddy, don't you think your Venus could use something to carry? Maybe, oh, I don't know, an enormous disembodied head?"

As they turned to go, all still giggling, May furled the paper up again and, not even looking our way, tossed it in a high smooth arc toward the window we were camped behind.

Mead, as if he'd known all along it was coming, caught it with a precise claw-snap. Ed and I just stared at each other. "Mead?" I finally ventured, "Did May . . . Was she aiming that at us?"

Mead only stared back with blank yellow eyes. I wasn't going to be the first to drop my gaze. Finally he looked away, and harrumphed into speech.

"It may be that May has more in common with you than you guess. Have you noticed she's always drawing along the edges of her father's sheets?"

I had, now that he said it. "Birds," I said suddenly. "And sheep, goats, even the occasional pig. But with—"

"Yes," Mead broke in, "animals with real expressions. Brooding pigeons. Irate pigs. Embarrassed chickens—how does she manage that?" He looked away again.

Finally he stared me straight in the face again and sniffed. "Well, it did occur to me that if I let her get a glimpse of me, she might feel"—he paused, took a breath,—"she might feel sorry for me. Even sorry enough to toss me something she thought I might want."

If I'd had a wing to pat Mead on the back at that moment, I would have used it. Instead, I leaned forward as if to get my balance, arms tight around Mead's neck. I don't think there were any words to make my feeling plainer.

CHAPTER TEN

fresh and fell

s we started what I guessed would be a long flight eastward to Iceland, I settled in to count how many more feathers Mead had lost. I was just about to open my mouth to ask Mead about the patches of white skin peeking through his glossy feathers when I felt Ed's pencil poking me in the back.

I turned around and saw that he had written on his notebook:

Approximate Feathers Lost per Jump: 3 6 ~~12 24 48 96~~ 192 (384) (768)

As I studied it, Ed vigorously underlined the *192* to make sure I got the point: That was the count right now.

I shook my head vigorously. *No way!* I mouthed to him, certain that I would have seen that many feathers fall off. Ed nodded solemnly and pointed behind him toward Mead's tail. He could be right, I realized with a lurch; I hadn't had a view behind Ed, and I'd have to trust him with the numbers. Now he was whispering something to me, leaning low so Mead couldn't hear: "This is not molting—this is balding." The word didn't scare me at first; it was almost a comfortable one, reminding me of my dad, or of Ed's cheerfully clueless English teacher. But then I got the drift. Bald men walk around with baseball caps; bald birds plummet to the ground.

I didn't like what I saw on Ed's page; I was a decent enough math student to know a geometric progression when I saw one. The feathers that Mead lost doubled every time. Two more trips and Mead would have lost more than fifteen hundred feathers. I tried not to think about what Mead must be suffering, what every little bump and sudden midair adjustment meant to his body. What if we hadn't come with him? If this had been his *geas* alone, I thought with a spasm of intense self-loathing, he'd probably be home and done by now. (*Probably?* a little voice said at once. *Do you really think he could have done alone what you all did together?*)

The important question now was, how many feathers could Mead lose and still be able to get where we needed to go? Ed was watching my face intently, so he could tell right away (brothers are like that) when I started asking myself that question. He flipped the page over and tapped again with his pencil, importantly.

The next page had fewer numbers on it.

Blackbird Feathers (educated guess): ~~750~~ ~~1,250~~ ~~1,500~~ 2,000 (?)

Feathers required to fly—?

I grabbed the pencil and, calling the poem back to mind, jotted quickly: *dragon, birds, hawthorn, Thames(?)*. The math seemed hopeless, but I went through the mental motions anyway. If there were four jumps left, not to mention whatever getting back home might take, then Mead was going to lose 3,072 feathers.

I reached up impetuously, scratched out Ed's *2,000* and wrote *5,000* in heavy black strokes, and underlined it for emphasis.

Ed looked at me silently and shook his head. Staring back at him, I nodded fiercely. Had to be. What other chance was there?

I lost track of the hours, waking and dozing, but Mead had eaten both those shriveled apples by the time we dropped through the clouds. I swallowed hard. We were gliding down toward the eeriest, wildest place I'd ever seen, floating above a wide green plain with a wind sweeping wildly across it, blowing two stunted trees nearly flat. That wasn't grass down there, it was some kind of soft mossy stuff, like a mix between Velcro and wool. At first, that was all I could make out.

"Where are we?" I couldn't help saying in awe.

Mead harrumphed weakly. "Summer glacial outcroppings," he began, "make it clear we're near the Arctic Circle." The crabbiness sounded unconvincing, almost scary in his newly faded voice. Still, I wasn't going to insult him by talking to him like an invalid.

"Oh thanks, Mead," I said tartly, hoping Ed would follow my lead. "So the Faroe Islands, maybe? Svalbard?" But Ed was staring around him like a madman, and I couldn't blame him. Close by on our left, a steep craggy mountain with a conical top gloomed over us; long daggers of ice shimmered down its sides the way melted ice cream drips down a sundae glass. After a minute, I spotted a pack of incredibly woolly sheep, baaing mournfully, huddled under an out-cropping at the base of the mountain.

Above them, I could just make out one bearded sturdy traveler leading a heavily laden little horse up a narrow crag, nearly at the mountain's top. Behind him rode a chubbier figure, swaddled in ani-mal skins. Everything had changed, thirty years had passed, and yet for just a second, struggling on the barrel-backed horse, Morris was a boy again. As we glided over him in the gathering gloom of evening, on a sudden whim I leaned crazily over Mead's wing and shouted down "Yoicks!" He looked around wildly and pawed at his belt, where the scabbard of his sword would have been.

Mead found us a boulder ("If there's one thing Iceland has, it's plenty of useful boulders," whispered Ed, reading my mind). We were no more than ten yards from where Morris and a companion with the same furs, big belt, and almost the same beard as Morris (Eiríkr, I guessed) were pitching their tent and digging into what looked to me like sides of raw fish. "Splendid! Like being inside a saga!" I heard Morris exclaim delightedly.

Ed was all efficiency now, zipping my bag up tight, fussing with his notebook, and quizzing Mead, as if we were on a Sunday picnic.

"Right! The next thing we need is 'a fork-tongued dragon fresh and fell.'" Ed was looking around as if he expected Mead to pluck it from the ground.

Mead pretended not to hear. Or maybe he really hadn't heard; he was getting a faraway look in his eyes now, the sort Granny sometimes got in front of the Tapestry. Which in a way, it suddenly occurred to me, was where we all were right now. My head hurt too much to pursue the thought.

"Do you like the looks of that horse Morris is currying right now?" Mead said in a soft voice; no Mary Poppins in it at all. "He's named Mouse. At the end of the trip Morris is so fond of him that he brings him home to that new house on the Thames, Kelmscott Manor. I wonder how many of the little gypsy horses you can see there nowadays have Mouse blood in them?"

"That's very funny, Mead, ha-ha-ha," said Ed, not listening at all and practically hopping with excitement. "But about the fork-tongued dragon?"

Mead reached out a long claw and snared a greasy fish bone Morris had tossed away. "I think," he remarked between repulsive bites, "that Eiríkr and William will likely start singing songs of Sigurd, who knew the tongues of birds and beasts. You could wake me when they start." With that he tucked his head under his wing.

So we waited. No choice—and no fish bones for us, either, I couldn't help noting grimly. That box of granola bars was a long time gone. Morris, after scribbling for a long time in his diary, went

to stand looking out over the plain at a range of steep, craggy moun-
tains to the north. One of them had a visible cone on top, glowing
red from what could only be lava inside. "Holy Tolkien, it's Mount
Doom!" whispered Ed in awe.

Although it was nearly freezing, it must have been June or July,
because as the shadows lengthened the sun stayed stubbornly over
the horizon. The breeze smelled like that spongy, bouncy turf, even
a little like the ocean. I remembered a trip we'd once taken up the
coast of Maine, where gray and black spears of rock dropped suddenly into the Atlantic.

"I'm coming back here someday," I promised myself.

And just like that, I saw the answer to my puzzle, why I'd felt
happy that we couldn't sell the Tapestry to the museum. When I
thought about what my life might be like when I grew up, it wasn't
Eva I thought of, or the school itself. Or even, if I was being honest,
Granny and Ed. What I thought about—and this is going to sound
really weird—was the Tapestry. What was happening in its forests;
what might be behind the mountain you could see in the back left
corner; mainly, what kind of life was going on in there.

It was so simple I found myself giggling. I'd felt glad that day
because I wanted the Tapestry all for myself. It's true I didn't want
Mr. Nazhar to take it, but not because I wanted Lexus guy to come
and take it away. Somehow, the Tapestry had gotten wrapped so
tightly into my life that there was no way I could imagine anyone
else standing before it.

"They can't take a look! No looks will be taken!" I found myself whispering, and I had to laugh at how fierce I sounded. It felt like a scab had given way. Only it still made me a terrible person, didn't it?

Then right below me (I'd completely forgotten he was there) I heard Morris say meditatively, as if he'd been daydreaming, "Yes, yes indeed, I'm coming back here someday. It's made me dream as I never thought I could dream." I tried not to breathe, hoping that Morris would go on talking.

"Do you know what, you old fish-breath?" Morris had roused himself a bit and poked Eiríkr awake. "I was dreaming of my love nest at home. Should I read you the poem I wrote?" Without waiting for an answer he pulled out a little fragment and began:

> "Dead and gone is all desire
> Gone and left me cold and bare
> Gone as the kings that few remember
> And their battle cry . . ."

Something friends of Morris learned: the gift of silence. Eiríkr held his breath a few minutes, waiting to see if there was any more. Then he unwrapped a book neatly wrapped in oilcloth and held it up to Morris with a questioning look.

Morris slid down next to him, and opened the book so it lay between them. "Yes, yes, a saga!" he exclaimed immediately. "*Sigurd the Volsung*, why not? That's my translation there, is it?"

Soon I heard them crooning softly, Eiríkr reciting in what must be Icelandic, then Morris after him in English.

At first it was hard to pick up the lilting syllables, but after a while I heard Morris say clearly, "What shall we do next? How about the dragon's bane, when Sigurd hides in a pit to slay the worm-tongue Fafnir?" Eiríkr turned some pages and resumed the moist burble of Icelandic (Ed: "He sounds like a drunk loon humming to himself underwater"). When Morris chimed in, however, it grew louder and fiercer:

Now crept the worm down to his place of watering, and the earth shook all about him, and he snorted forth venom on all the way before him as he went; but Sigurd neither trembled nor was adrad at the roaring of him.

"*Adrad?*" I heard Eiríkr ask. "Why not just terrified?" Morris only held up a warning hand and went right on:

So whenas the worm crept over the pits, Sigurd thrust his sword under his left shoulder, so that it sank in up to the hilts; then up leapt Sigurd from the pit and drew the sword back again unto him, and therewith was his arm all bloody, up to the very shoulder.

"And that," shouted Morris triumphantly, jumping up so the book would have tumbled to the ground if Eiríkr hadn't snagged it in midair, "is one dead dragon, by Wotan!" Ed laughed under his breath, but I couldn't join in. As Morris had been reciting the story, the queasiest feeling had come over me, as if my own arm were covered with dragon gore.

I punched my leg in bewilderment. First I thought I was Morris;
now I was starting to feel like a character in one of his stories. Mead
seemed to have some idea what was happening to me, but I sure
didn't.

Suddenly I heard Ed's laughter stop. He pointed a shaky hand
at the ground below us. There was a kind of vibration in the air, the
kind you can sometimes see above a fire—and I caught a whiff of that
same sweet smell from the moment we hit the Tapestry. As we sat
there watching, only feet from where Morris and Eiríkr sat chanting
from the sagas, a dragon shimmered into being. It was like watching
a dream come alive—except that this dragon had the gruesome chest
wound the saga described.

"Fresh and fell," I whispered; and once I started shivering I didn't
stop. This was obviously a job for Mead. I looked down at him, head
not quite hidden under his wing; the feathers that should have concealed him completely now formed only an imperfect veil. He was
still the biggest and the most experienced of us all. Clearly if anyone
was going to tackle this dragon, the job was his. Ed started to tug at
his wing. "See it, Mead?" he was whispering.

For some reason, though, I found myself standing up. Before I
even heard Mead's bemused "What? What do you see, Ed?" I was
moving out from the cover of the boulder, trying to silence the voice
screaming at me to run back and bury my head under Mead's wing.
Rather than walking right at a dragon so huge, and so hot, that I
could even feel my arm hairs starting to curl.

Thick black smoke was still pouring from the nostrils that lay

just above its terrifying razor teeth, but strangely enough I found myself wondering exactly how much bigger it was than the elephant I'd once patted at Roger Williams Zoo. My pulse was steady, and my mind was busy with logistics. *Will it fold up when I touch it? Or will I have to use my pocketknife to hack out the forked tongue?* One way or another, I had no doubt that there was going to be room in our bag for whatever the Tapestry needed. There just had to be. I squared my shoulders, and set to work.

CHAPTER ELEVEN

The People Marching On

"**C**an we check on Mouse first when we get back?" Ed was saying to Mead as we plunged back over England, its tidy green fields and low rolling hills unfolding comfortingly under us. I knew he was doing his best to pretend nothing was wrong, trying to get Mead's mind off his lost feathers and increasingly labored breathing.

But I could also tell that what we'd just gone through had meant less to Ed than it did to me. He'd shaken off Iceland quicker than I had, probably hadn't even heard my vow to come back. I wondered if he would be with me when I went back there one day. Could I herd sheep, I found myself wondering. Or find a way to make a living fishing, pushing a small boat out every day into that steely gray surf? Images from those little villages we'd flown over stuck with me like a slide show, floating in front of my face even as the ground beneath us grew dense with people, crowded with traffic.

"We got it!" Ed chirped up suddenly. "We're really almost there." I nodded and smiled. But as I did the same mental arithmetic that Ed had been doing (four to go?), it struck me that in Iceland something had changed. I had stopped caring what we found. Or at least stopped caring in the same way.

Oh great! What else was I going to find out about myself? Not only was I a selfish hoarder, I also didn't care about art, and what made a *real* work of art. But that was it, I realized. No matter how much Granny knew about Morris and Company, there was a basic fact about the Tapestry she'd completely missed.

It wasn't Morris's signature that made it an artwork, and it never had been. A collectible, maybe, or a valuable way to pay for our house. But what made it art was something else again. If the life came into it when I looked, what did it matter if it was an original or a copy, or just something that some other weaver had put together a hundred or fifty years ago? Or yesterday, for that matter. The professors might care, and the curators, but I didn't—and I had a sneaking suspicion that Morris wouldn't have cared, either.

So what were we doing here? It occurred to me that I had an answer for that, too. I didn't care about getting the trustees to believe the Tapestry was genuine. Whether it made us money or not, whether it made the museum happy or not, I wanted to see those Lost Spots filled. "Come back!" I found myself whispering ferociously, "Oh, come back!"

Ed poked me. He'd scribbled something on the pad he was shoving at me: *Maybe it's only the Jumps that take feathers!* Out loud, what he said was "Don't worry, Jen, when we land we can take as much time as we want to find the singing birds in the town of the tree."

I nodded. It made sense to focus on the quest one step at a time; what else could we do at this point? Maybe Mead had only three flights left in him, or even two. But maybe there was some power we didn't know about, some way to heal him.

Suddenly, without thinking about it, as if it just had to come out, I opened my mouth and said, "Mead, is there any medicine for you?"

Though Mead kept his head turned away, I could tell just from the set of his neck that he understood the question right away. He didn't pretend not to know, didn't make me show him Ed's notebook calculations. After a long pause, he said, "Well, there may be. There is a place, a spot enclosed by willows beside the Thames. But there's no reaching it until this quest is done; no way at all."

I felt the blood pounding under my skin; we had to find that spot, and right away. The quest could wait, and . . .

But Mead was going on. "Children, I'm old but not yet blind. Could I have snatched what Ed has snatched? Woken myself to face that dragon? None of what I thought I lived for could have been done without you."

"But Mead . . ." I couldn't help the desperate whining note I heard in my voice, like a girl about to cry. But that girl absolutely could *not* be me.

"Have you considered," he went on, his cranky whisper a faint echo of his voice only a few jumps back, "how many times I have tried to enter that Tapestry to accomplish what I thought was my duty? Considered that nobody ever told me I had a *geas;* that even the strongest roc only matters to the story because of where he takes Sinbad?"

Ed and I looked at each other in dismay, and Mead finally said, heavily, "Have you considered, in fact, that you two are the heroes of this adventure? And that at best I can be nothing more than a minor character?"

Had I considered it? It was worse even than that. I'd never stopped thinking about myself as a hero—no, as *the* hero of this adventure. I didn't need Mead to explain to me what that meant. Whether I was thinking I was Morris or thinking I knew what it felt like to slay the dragon, I was in the heart of things—maybe for the first time in my life. Even saving Mead seemed to be part of *my* mission. There seemed to be nothing to say. We trundled on in silence: companionable or uneasy, I wasn't quite sure which.

After an hour or so, Mead finally threw a glance back over his shoulder. "So," he said with a pleased croak, "I suppose you two philosophers are too busy to notice that I just performed a perfect one-claw landing on top of a London omnibus?"

◆　　◆　　◆

The bus, drawn by a pair of silent chestnut workhorses, slowly traveled west through central London at sunset. Ed and I peeked down though an open window to see a beaming William Morris, grayer and definitely fatter but otherwise unmistakably himself. He was energetically haranguing the person at his side. For a minute I thought it was Jane. Then she gave a familiar jerk of the arm, William Morris style: it could only be May. Dressed like a young lady, yet barely up to his shoulder. A child still, but rushing to become . . . well, somebody. I could almost count the lines between her eyes as she peered intently across the aisle, following her father's gaze.

May was staring at a tall, mildlooking man with light hair and a droopy mustache. You'd have bet he was a librarian, or maybe a veterinarian—even from here I could see the tufts of cat hair clinging to his shabby tweed jacket. Oblivious to the sway of the car, he clung to his little brown clothbound book with white knuckles, lips moving slightly.

Morris, all jumps and twitches and triumphant glances, couldn't stand it any longer. Leaning across the aisle, he put his stubby finger on the book's open page and started reciting loudly.

> "Folk say, a wizard to a northern king
> At Christmastide such wondrous things did show,
> That through one window men beheld the spring,
> And through another saw the summer glow,
> And through a third the fruited vines arow."

The man twitched violently and jumped as if waking up from a dream. He looked at his book, looked at Morris, then looked down at his book again and in a shaky voice continued:

> *"While still, unheard, but in its wonted way,*
> *Piped the drear wind of that December day."*

Morris chimed in now and they went on together, Morris waving his arms as if he were conducting an orchestra.

> *"So with this Earthly Paradise it is,*
> *If ye will read aright, and pardon me,*
> *Who strive to build a shadowy isle of bliss*
> *Midmost the beating of the steely sea."*

May was blushing furiously by now and looking frantically around, probably for a pit to crawl into. The people nearby, though, behaved as if the evening ride was incomplete without at least one tag-team recitation of epic poetry. Somebody yawned, two or three gentlemen refolded their newspapers. One small boy started laughing, got shushed instantly by a bossy older sister, and subsided.

The man reached up to remove his hat, discovered he wasn't actually wearing one, and blushed. "Sir," he started, got embarrassed, cleared his throat. Tried again. "Sir, I recognize your face from this evening's Socialist Guild meeting. May I introduce myself? Emery Walker, by trade a printer."

Ed jiggled next to me deliriously. "It's Photogravure Walker!" he whispered ecstatically.

"Shut up, techno-freak!" I whispered furiously back. Walker was still speaking.

"I take it," he went on, "that like me you are an ardent admirer of *The Earthly Paradise* by the great poet William Morris?"

"None greater!" bellowed Morris with an exuberant laugh. Grabbing Walker's arm, he propelled him down the steps, counting on the driver to lurch to a stop (he did).

"Well, Mr. Emery Walker, printer, shall we walk and talk? Tonight I feel not only an ardent revolutionary but also, thanks to you, a very happy man. Let's build our own socialist isle of bliss."

May grabbed the bulky box he'd left behind: "I'll just tuck these magic lantern slides away at home and check on Jenny." As the bus turned out of sight, we heard the occasional word float back down the street: "Father . . . issue . . . *Commonweal* . . . proofreading . . . !" And a final despairing wail, "Remember!" It had the sound of something she yelled at him a lot.

As they strolled along bustling Oxford Street in the gathering shades of evening, Morris and Walker were soon deep in talk. So deep we were able to glide cautiously along behind them, tree to tree, never falling out of earshot. Morris was bouncing on the balls of his feet, sawing the air so vigorously that Walker kept having to swerve to avoid a punch in the nose.

He was talking about his trip to Iceland; suppers he'd shared in the poorest little fishing villages. "The most grinding poverty is a trifling evil, Walker, compared with the inequality of classes." Waving an arm so wildly that Walker had no choice but to duck into a butcher's doorway. As Morris strolled obliviously down the street, Emery struggled to disentangle himself from dangling coils of sausage under the butcher's baleful glare.

"Listening to those fishermen talk to me about saga heroes like Njall and Sigurd as if they'd performed their heroic deeds last week, I got a glimpse of what we stand to gain if, if . . ." Finally noticing Walker far behind, Morris reluctantly spluttered to a halt for as long as it took him to pull within earshot.

Morris had put on what I was beginning to think of as his stare into the future: a thousand-yard stare. He wasn't talking to Walker now, but to some imaginary audience. "In Iceland," he began with a little wave of the hand that made Walker look behind him nervously (I giggled; he was checking to see if Morris might be talking to a quick-gathering crowd of listeners), "I began to see socialism through the eyes of an artist. We are practitioners of the lesser arts—our weaving, wallpapers, our tiles, even these illuminated manuscripts. Though we sell to the wealthy, our art can have no real growth but life under commercialism and profit-mongering. If it doesn't belong to everybody, it's nothing, and nobody's."

Walker's voice was so low I missed it, but he must have been asking Morris something about how he'd written *The Earthly Paradise.* "It was all done at the loom, Walker!" In nearby trees, birds flew up at the sound of his voice, thought better of it, settled back to roost. "If a chap can't compose an epic poem while he's weaving tapestry, he had better shut up; he'll never do any good at all."

Suddenly I recognized the open space they were heading toward: "Trafalgar Square!" I whispered to Ed, "That must be Nelson's Column." I saw Ed's blank stare—naval history is one of his few weaknesses. "They built it when Lord Nelson smashed Napoleon's navy off Spain."

I'd always wanted to see Nelson up on his column. But when Morris looked angrily up at Nelson, I suddenly saw him differently. True happiness lay in sinking the enemy, the admiral's blank stare proclaimed; what other joy could there be? In Morris's eyes, Nelson wasn't so much a hero as another expert killer, someone who trained his men to blast French sailors with the finest cannons British factories could build him. It struck me: How many statues were there to Morris and people like him—people whose victories didn't involve gunpowder and corpses?

I could hear Morris describing a recent protest. "Only three dead after the police came in, the papers reported. *Only* three! How many would they have liked?"

"Bloody Sunday, I heard it called," said Walker meditatively, rubbing the toe of his sturdy leather boot along a rusty stain on the pavement.

Rather than answering, Morris started to hum. "There's an American song that's been running through my head, Walker, perhaps you know it?" The tune he hummed was incredibly familiar to me. Ed tugged my sleeve, leaned forward, and whispered, "It's 'John Brown's

Body Lies a-Mouldering in the Grave'! You know, the anti-slavery version of 'The Battle Hymn of the Republic.'" He started to sing: "Mine eyes have seen the glory of the coming of the Lord . . ."

I hushed him: Morris was going on. "I don't quite have it right yet, Walker, but something like this.

> *"What is this, the sound and rumour? What is this that all men*
>   *hear,*
> *Like the wind in hollow valleys when the storm is drawing near,*
> *Like the rolling on of ocean in the eventide of fear?*
> *'Tis the people marching on."*

Walker smiled encouragingly; an *I'll just nip down and give the cat a treat* kind of smile. In response, Morris gave a pleased grunt (if Morris were a big tabby cat, he'd have purred). "I tell you, Walker, all the lectures in the world, all the lantern slides, are not going to rouse the people to change their government."

"Yes," piped up Walker unexpectedly, "I sometimes think the government is more likely to change the people than the other way around."

Morris plowed ahead. "So we'll have to try something else, won't we?" Walker nodded tentatively, not quite sure where this was heading—a look I'd come to recognize in the faces of Ned, Janey, Webb, even Rossetti.

"What I mean, Walker, is this: What if I could write songs that would tell the real working people of this country—every country for that matter—who they really are, what they've done and what they might yet do?" Walker nodded slowly, eyes still locked on Morris's face.

"Listen to this, tell me what you think!" Without waiting for an answer, Morris launched into another verse, still to the same tune:

"These are they who build thy houses, weave thy raiment, win
   thy wheat,
Smooth the rugged, fill the barren, turn the bitter into sweet,
All for thee this day—and ever. What reward for them is meet
Till the host comes marching on?

"What do you say, Mr. Walker, might we get this echoing in their ears? Do the workers more good in their mouths than anything from a book!"

Walker laughed politely, then paused, about to take a risk. "Well, Morris," he said, testing the formulation carefully: Could he really address someone twenty years his senior by his last name, like a schoolboy? "The thing is, Morris," he said again, bolder this time, "you weren't made to sing, you know." He blushed deeply ("Quite right," muttered Mead, "dreadful voice!") but hurried on: "You were made to, to, to, make books."

Morris, who'd been humming the tune over and over as Walker spoke, broke off suddenly. "By heavens, Walker," he shouted so suddenly that Walker started violently, "there's no disputing it! We should make books. Right!"

Walker gave a startled look around him as if he expected Morris to pull a printing press out of his pocket. "Back to Kelmscott House!" Morris barked, giving Walker a brisk clap (a buffet, really) on the back. "Do you suppose we can have a Chaucer ready by Christmas?"

I hitched my bag expectantly and turned to Mead. Wouldn't we follow them? Ed, though, was peering intently up into the tree we were perched in: to judge from the acorns all around us, a red oak. "Beside the dark hills," he was muttering, looking around at the looming London buildings that hemmed us in. "The dark hills . . . the town of the tree."

"The town?" I was puzzled. "How is a tree a town?"

Instead of answering, Mead, too, recited softly: "All birds sing in the town of the tree." I felt a little shiver building. Morris was speed-ing away from us, out of earshot already. But here we sat, in a grimy London tree, waiting for what?

I turned for reassurance to Ed. Reasonable level-headed Ed, who'd never climbed a tree in his life, let alone a fifty-foot oak in the dark. He was looking up over our heads, intently studying the trembling leaves. Even the trunk was vibrating faintly. I'd thought it was just me shivering, but now I realized that the sun was setting, and all over the tree birds were moving, flicking their wings, getting ready for, for what? Something that only happened at dusk.

"Mead," I whispered, trying to calm down. "Mead? What's going on with Ed? Does he know what he's doing?" Ed turned to look at me and gave me a little absentminded smile. Then, before

I could say anything, he was up and into the leaves, swinging himself up on branches that looked far too frail to bear his weight. As he disappeared from sight above us, the birds all started to sing at once.

There was a long period when I could hear nothing but the singing, louder and louder. We hadn't eaten for a long time, I found myself thinking. And then a second later, "I wonder what Granny made for dinner?"

I could have kicked myself. People didn't think about what Granny made for dinner when they were under a *geas*. Or did they?

I snuck a quick glance over at Mead. In his face at that moment, there was no quest, no William Morris—he didn't even look like a teacher. I wondered what was showing on my own face. I gave it a quick wipe, looked down at my palm. Paint from Rossetti's mural, a black smudge from ducking through a skylight at the Red House, coal grime, and, right over my lip, a thick, gleaming red liquid from Iceland that could only be . . . I shuddered again. Mead looked over and muttered sleepily, "Fafnir found when he tasted it he could speak with animals."

"It?"

Mead looked at me hard. Suddenly I could feel all those splotches on my face and neck start to pulse and sting. "Do you need me to tell you what splattered your face in Iceland?"

I sat there thinking, listening to the singing above us, wishing, as hard as I'd wished for anything in my life, for Ed to come crunching and thudding back down through the branches to us. Without even thinking about it, I put the smear to my mouth and licked it. Nothing, nothing happened.

"Mead!" I said. No reply. "Mead! I can't hear them!" Mead looked at me brightly. "What's happening up there?" He still didn't say anything. I could feel the tang of whatever that was in my mouth: salty, and a little sweet. I was suddenly extremely hungry, and tired. Most of all, like an itch I wasn't allowed to scratch, I missed Granny.

Then suddenly there he was, pushing through the branches above our head in the dusk: a sneaker, a leg, then, after a long pause, his hoodie was shoved down at us without a word. It was . . . "Squirming!" I hissed in alarm. "Ed, your hoodie is squirming!"

"Actually," said Ed drily, "my hoodie right now is singing, in the town of the tree." And sure enough, very faintly through the sweaty, grimy cloth, I could hear a chirrup, then another and another. I tried not to think about how that little ball of songbirds would make its way onto the Tapestry. Maybe Mead would have an idea.

Ed took a deep sigh, and something about it made me look him straight in the eyes. For what felt like a very long time, but might have been only a few seconds, he stared straight back at me. I couldn't remember the last time he'd done that. "You look . . ." I trailed off.

Ed smiled a little, but only with his eyes. "I look just like you did, Jen, when you came back with that forked tongue for the Tapestry."

He reached out to wipe something I'd missed off my cheek, his touch as sure and smooth as Granny's. "Should we go, Mead?" he said, with exactly the tone of voice I'd been looking for all along.

Like James Bond, I told myself fuzzily. "Next stop, Kelmscott Manor, I think?"

Mead, without comment, dropped us into London's gathering dark. In a minute or two I felt Ed go heavy next to me; his breathing evened out into the steady slow metronome I remembered from a long time ago. As I drifted away after him, barely aware of Mead's back, Ed's side, or even my precious bag, I thought I could hear the birds singing beside me. I could almost make out the words they were singing. "'Tis the people marching on," I whispered from the bottom of a deep, black well.

CHAPTER TWELVE

for My Sake

I woke up with a question. "He's wrong, isn't he, Mead?"

We were still drifting slowly along the Thames as the sun rose behind us in the east. Either Kelmscott was farther than I thought, or Mead was slowing down. *Focus on what's going right,* I told myself firmly. At least Ed was still asleep.

Mead tilted his head without comment. "About socialism, I mean. We live in a commercial profit-mongering world, too, right? And Morris was wrong to think art could do anything to change that."

Mead opened his beak, tilted his head, and then shut it again with a click and looked at me inquiringly. *Go on.* "If Morris had been right about what art could do, or what it could make people see, then the world would be a fairer place, wouldn't it? Granny wouldn't keep talking to that Lexus guy, and thinking about all the money he'd give her to have our things for his private collection."

Mead stayed mute, so I went on. "And Granny wouldn't be making all those late-night phone calls about . . ."

I looked over at Ed to make sure he was still asleep. His eyes were still closed, but as I turned back he broke in suddenly, his voice calm as always: "About the foster home Aunt Cathy thinks we should go to?"

I swallowed hard. Still, I was almost glad. Somehow I didn't feel like hiding those calls from the new Ed, who climbed up into the town of the tree, even looked me in the eye occasionally, and who talked to Mead like James Bond consulting another secret agent. It made it easier for me to say what I wanted to now.

"Granny made the same mistake as Morris, didn't she, Mead? She thought that art had some special power, something different about it than the prices it brings at auction. But look at our house, our basically empty house, and what's going to happen to us now. What good did art ever do her?"

"And if I told you," Mead said slowly, looking up ahead toward the thin line of the Thames on the horizon, "that Morris thought art was a picture of how we might live, of how we ought to live, instead of how we do live?"

For some reason, as he spoke I found myself remembering what it felt like to make my arm, trembling and cold, reach down into the dragon's mouth.

"Well." I took a deep breath. "Morris said art proved that everyone in the world shares 'equality of condition.' Whatever you undergo is something that might happen to me. For Morris, that meant every jolt of pain you feel should bother me, and vice versa. But"—I spoke slowly here, puzzling it out—"the same rule should also apply for joy: Yours is mine and mine is yours."

As I said this, some of Morris's pictures flashed into my mind: tall ladies riding through forests beside god-like knights; little birds coiled into a trellis, or dipping low over a river where it bent away into the forest.

"We live in a world where the best things don't happen—where planes crash, and people go into foster homes for no good reason." I tried to say it without shaking too much. "But no matter what world you live in," I went on doggedly, "art tells a different story. It's the dragon at your feet—and it's also the volcano everyone can catch sight of on the horizon. It's what lets us rehearse the right life. No matter how wrong the one we're living in right now feels."

Ed looked up at me with a hard-to-read expression: Temptation, maybe? Pain? He broke in. "So Jen, did Granny do the right thing not to sell her collection to Lexus guy? Even if it means our lives are going to be, to be . . ." He trailed off.

I looked to Mead for a hint. His breath came hard as he descended toward Kelmscott Manor, and there was far more skin than feather showing now along his back. Saying nothing.

"I think it's Granny's job to do what's best—for us, I mean, not just for the art she made or kept. But I also think—" I paused for a long time, so long that Mead craned his head around almost backward to stare into my eyes. "—that maybe seeing her do what's right for everyone really is what's best for us. So maybe when she sold those things to the museum instead of seeing what Lexus guy would pay, that was another way of teaching us. Think of all the other ways she's taught us over the years: when she made us knit with her, and sew, and even"—I looked down at my blistered fingers—"solder. If what we do is only for ourselves, then what are we?"

Ed leaned forward, too intent on answering to notice he was crushing me up against Mead's neck. "Okay, fine, Jen, but what good is that if we lose the house? If we have to go off to I don't know where with I don't know who, so we're not a family anymore!"

Sneaking a glance down at the newest page in his notebook, I could see just two words, written over and over: *And Mead? And Mead? And Mead?* We rode a gentle thermal high above the Thames, heading for an old house that glowed gold and warm gray in the noon sun. Nobody said a word.

Just before we coasted to a halt on a stone wall streaked with gray-green lichen, Ed came back to life. "Remember, next is 'the white-flowered hawthorn brake,'" he whispered urgently. "A brake's a thicket, so that's what we need to find."

It was hard for me to drag myself back into the world of the poem.

How long ago had it been that we'd heard Granny recite it? Two days for us, or three maybe? And how long for the world we'd left behind? I shuddered and decided not to think about it.

When I heard the laughter coming over the wall, though, the poem's next line popped straight into my head: "Love be merry for my sake." What else would you call it but merry, the sight of May trying to clamber on Topsy's back while Jane popped an old white hat over the ears of a horse that could only be Mouse? Even Jenny, reclining near Ned in the shade, had a little smile on today. Like a fancy dress only brought out for parties, it lit her up.

Best of all by far, though, was to see the lawn littered with heavy oak tables—"the same ones Philip Webb made for the Red House," I whispered just as Mead opened his beak, for the sheer pleasure of watching him shut it again with a click. Ed gave a giggle that sounded much more like his eleven-year-old self.

All over those tables were spread gorgeous sheets of parchment, weighted down by heavy old pen cases, brass boxes, and the occasional rock. Each sheet was absolutely covered with drawings by Morris.

"He's on to something new!" I whispered to Ed, who was busily scanning the garden for traces of hawthorn among the roses. Meanwhile I was soaking it all in. There was a snug wooden gazebo lodged solidly against one of the garden's old gray walls and a medlar tree with its UFO-shaped purple fruit. And that carefully pruned yew hedge: I gulped hard and fought down an irrational stab of fear. I recognized its low, sinuous, sinister shape, even before I saw the curling label in May's handwriting: HERE BEE FAFNIR, THE DRAGONNE.

Suddenly we were moving again. "Mead, I don't think you should . . . ," I said in alarm, but it was too late. Choosing a moment when everyone was watching May try to topple her father to the ground, Mead neatly sped us low along the grass. Though we were trailing feathers behind us like smoke, and though I could feel his muscles trembling beneath my clutching knees, a second later we were tucked underneath one of the tables. We were just barely concealed under the trailing edge of a long linen curtain Jane was hemming at one side of the table.

Ed started an indignant dumb-show, pointing out at the dark corners of the garden where he could start hunting for a hawthorn brake. Mead, eyes closed meditatively, didn't seem to be listening. He muttered something very quietly ("yearning friend"?) and then seemed to go very still, all at once.

There was a tumult of voices overhead, then the ponies settled down to graze and their riders turned slowly back to work. Every-thing, even Morris (miracle of miracles), went quiet for a while. Ed was studying the final few lines of the poem intently, lips moving, and I was just beginning to drift off for a little nap. Mouse, I noticed drowsily, seemed to have sniffed us, because he was beginning to amble across the lawn, his big brown eyes mostly obscured by the daisy chain that Janey had woven into his overgrown mane.

Suddenly I heard May hopping up and down chanting "Papa! Papa! *Papa!* Does this cross-stitch look right to you?" If in London with her box of slides she'd been the boss-in-training, here at Kelm-scott she was still an overgrown girl.

Instead of answering, Morris gave a deep bearish growl, and (to judge from the whoops) was attempting to toss May, who must have been nearly his height by now, up into the air.

"When I was young, my little Mayday, do you know where my parents sent me? Do you?" A pleased laugh was the only answer. "To nurses, then to gardeners, to grooms I seem to recall. They sent me . . . anywhere where *they* weren't. They, they farmed me out! Yes, I was sent to a . . ."

"A boy-farm!" shouted May and Jenny together.

"Yes, yes," said Morris, while what we could see of May's embroidery (he must have given up on tossing May herself) shot higher and higher in the air. "And on the dreaded Sundays spent home with my parents, when I failed my weekly spelling test as usual, they made me stand . . ."

"Barefoot on a chair!" chorused the girls triumphantly.

"William, my goodness, she's too old for that!" I heard someone calling faintly from the distant chairs.

"Right you are, Queen Jane!" called back Morris. "And that, burdens of my premature old age"—Morris tucked May's embroidery back down promptly on the bench with a surprisingly deft flourish—"is why we have brought you down to this lowlands country. To cut your hands on the weeping willows by the Thames and get soaked gathering knots of lush marsh-marigolds."

"And your gold illuminations, Papa?" came May's voice, almost above us now. (*Don't step on Mead's wing!* I silently beamed my thought at her.) Instead of answering, Morris snorted, and growled back deep in his throat.

"No matter how many infernally delicate and wrinkled sheets of gold leaf, it won't come right, May, not at all." Morris gave a flourish with his hand and a little snowfall drifted slowly to the grass, page after page of parchment falling around us. Mouse gave a startled snort. After a moment's somber reflection he began meditatively munching away at the nearest sheet. One long slender ribbon of paper, festooned with gold, green, and red, fell right into our hiding spot. Mead didn't stir. Without thinking, without even letting myself feel scared, I reached forward right between May's and Jenny's busy hands and grabbed it. Below a drawing of white flowers and small shiny green leaves, Morris had written in flowing medieval script, *In the white-flowered hawthorn brake.* I shoved it into my bag.

"Wake up, Mead!" I hissed urgently; the girls were going to find us any minute, and Mouse, paper dripping from his moving jaws, still hadn't ceased his steady amble toward us. I found myself wondering if he somehow smelled Iceland on us, or dragon blood? Ed was holding up his notebook over us, as if that could hide us when the whole family had started drifting in toward the table.

Everything had slowed way down. Mead shifted his head in the smallest possible way and murmured the same thing he'd said before. Trying to ignore the sound of the hunt raging above us, I bent my head close and listened intently. "Journey's end," Mead was

whispering, over and over, "journey's end." Then even the whispering stopped. Everything seemed to stop.

"Jen," Ed was saying, and shaking my shoulder over and over. I looked up expecting to find startled grown-ups looking down at us. I tried to dry my tears and think what to say to them: *Please, can we live in your century? If you like we can tell you about how badly everything turned out.*

When I looked up at last, though, the shouting had died away. There was only Ed looking down at me. And next to him, with late-afternoon light streaming in behind, her red hair loose so it glowed like fire, was the only person I could bear seeing me at that moment.

I reached toward her with a sob. My arms were clutched tight around my sweet mother's waist, and my head was buried in her shoulder. Then I heard Ed saying, "Jen, this is Jane Morris, Jane Burden Morris. I think she's going to help us." And I felt an arm go around me tightly and hold on. I felt the way a toy must feel when it's picked up, dusted off, and put back in the box for the night.

CHAPTER THIRTEEN

Journey's End

 I woke up on smooth warm hay. Prickly and dry, smelling like grass but packed solid under me: had to be hay. Which meant—my eyes shot open; a hay-loft. Yup, morning sun was lighting up one side of the barn below me, and above were only the crisscrossed timbers that supported a high-pitched slate roof.

I could feel the dried tears all over my face even before I opened my eyes. I lay there for a second on my side, preparing an apology to Ed, ready to tell him anything he needed to know. He had a right to understand why I'd gone to pieces when Mead died.

I gave a deep sigh and rolled over into a kneeling position. Tried to, anyway; there was something blocking my way. Something big and dark and warm against my body. As I opened my eyes to figure out what it was, someone said irritably, "I beg your pardon." Not just someone, but a huge, largely featherless bird wedged right up against me.

"Mead!" I shrieked. "But you're . . ."

"Very, very tired," Mead broke in gently, "and so I still am." The wing that reached out to tap me had barely a feather on it.

I was still trying to take it all in. "You said 'Journey's end,' Mead. And I thought—"

"You thought that Mead was giving a deathbed soliloquy, like a knight from a romance," broke in Ed suddenly. "Let me see, Jen, have you *ever* been wrong . . . ? Hmmm, let me get back to you on that." Pointing out my mistakes was as close as Ed ever came to teasing me. And I didn't have the slightest desire to argue the point.

"Oh, Mead," I said, and it sounded so good I said it again. "Oh, Mead." Nothing could be better than a living Mead.

Still, I couldn't help turning the phrase over and over in my mind. Journey's end, okay, so our journey was ended. But there was still "Thames runs chill . . ."

"So *journey's end* means . . . ," I said cautiously.

"That my flying days are done," said Mead promptly, in a tone as final as he'd used when discussing his bent claw. "Anything you gather from now on will not rely on a flying bird."

"But how . . . ," I started again, uncomfortably aware that I'd somehow gotten in the habit of starting sentences I was counting on other people to finish.

"Because we're here, Jen, at 'the old house by the Thames to which the people of the story went.'" Ed said it fast enough that I knew it must be a quotation from something, but at that moment my head was too muzzy to place it.

"This is it," he added, "Kelmscott Manor. Don't you get it?" he went on excitedly when I kept staring at him blankly, my mind whirling pointlessly like a machine that's slipped a gear. "We can do the rest on foot, because sooner or later everybody comes here. We just have to wait—"

"But Ed," I broke in gently, "we can't wait. This place may seem almost perfect." I took a second to smell the sweetness of the hay, to look up into the big loft and listen to the Thames chuckling nearby. "But Granny needs us back home."

I could tell Ed was getting ready to argue about what "now" meant exactly, so I switched gears. "Besides," I said, rubbing a hand shyly along Mead's side where a few glossy feathers still clung, "how could we stay here anyway? It's not as if Morris and his family are going to—"

Ed interrupted me again. "But that's the great part, Jen! Who do you think helped me get you and Mead into this old barn? Jane did it; she sent everyone else off on some crazy herb hunt in the meadows so they wouldn't spot you. You should have *seen* Morris leading the procession, the poor sap! He didn't suspect a thing. Then she set us up here, where nobody ever goes, and showed me where the apple barrels are, and a well we can sneak out to at night. She even found a little wicker cage for those birds I had tied up in my hoodie—I mean, the two who were still little enough not

to fly away—the ones I'm still"—he blushed—"hand-feeding with crickets and worms."

Ed looked up excitedly, and the blush faded from his face. "Plus we can start looking for that place by the Thames, where Mead can—"

"That's quite enough of that," said Mead, with a flash of his old sharpness. "There's no spot that will do any good before this quest is done." Ed's face, glimpsed briefly over Mead's shoulder, though, told a different story. We were going to find it, or go crazy trying.

And after a minute, I had to admit that Ed was right. At least, I made the mental reservation, he was right for now, until I could come up with something to get us home faster. I could see from the way different emotions flitted across his face that Ed still had something else on his mind. After a minute he circled back to it. "She's so nice, Jen," he said finally. "I was always scared of her when we were spying on her, because of how sad she looked. But up close, she . . ." He paused, puzzled.

I knew exactly what was coming. The Ed who climbed trees without looking down and figured out how to care for baby birds was not the same little boy I'd protected from all conversations about our dead parents. Still, I didn't want to talk about it right now. There would be time enough, later.

"She, she reminded me of—"

"I'm going to tell you who she reminded you of someday," I said quickly. "I promise you that."

Mead broke into the conversation now, his voice deeper and slower than before, but recognizably himself. "Ed's come up with the only plausible plan. If I can't fly, and there's no clear way home, what can we do but wait and see what comes to us?"

He inclined his head toward an appetizing bushel basket near at hand. "And really, Jen, there's no point in visiting England if you don't take advantage of the excellent apples. These are Bramleys, I believe, and Cox's Orange Pippins."

I looked at the two of them, smiling at each other; Ed was already munching noisily. "Oh, I give up," I said, reaching for one myself. "Just tell me when you two gourmets are ready to get back to some good honest thievery."

It took me a day or so tucked away in the lower barn at Kelmscott to realize it, but I was happy now. Happier than I'd been since I turned fourteen, happier maybe than I'd been since . . . since we came to live with Granny. But why? Hadn't I decided that my feelings about the Tapestry made me a bad person? Here we were hunting high and low for the details we could use to prove the Tapestry really was by Morris—but I'd somehow made up my mind that it really belonged to me after all. Didn't that make me a hoarder, too? As bad as Lexus guy? Trudging down the Thames one afternoon—we were still hunting for that perfect spot by the willows, whenever Mead wasn't watching us—I tried to understand what I'd been feeling about the Tapestry, and going home to Granny, and even about Eva.

I had a new kind of possessive feeling about the Tapestry now. *It's all mine,* I said over and over, but it didn't make me feel gross and guilty, the way I'd feel if I stole a dessert from Ed's plate, or if I got to watch a movie at night without him. This was different. I definitely had the Tapestry now (nobody could be closer to it than this, right?), but I wasn't robbing anybody. It was like owning it without depriving anybody else of it; as if it belonged to me in the same way that it could belong to anybody at all, if they decided to think about it the same way. But how could that be? Only one person I knew could explain that.

"Mead," I said that night at the barn after Ed had fallen asleep, "do you remember how I knew what Morris was feeling when he was making wallpaper?" Mead grunted faintly. Not an encouraging noise, but I plowed on.

"And you said of course I knew." Another grunt.

"But that's all you said," I finished awkwardly. Silence.

"Well," I finally went on, "I want to talk about why I would have known."

Had Mead fallen asleep? Or did his silence mean, *Well, it's a free country; talk away?*

I took a deep breath. "I was trying to figure out why I don't feel guilty for feeling so—" I paused, looking for the right word. "—so possessive about the Tapestry. When I think about these meadows, or about the dragon, or even little things like the ship with shields before the sun, I get this feeling they belong to me the same way my arms do. That's weird, right?"

Still nothing from Mead. So I took another breath and continued. "And then there's this other thing. It suddenly struck me that I didn't care who believed the Tapestry was by William Morris—like Morris's signature wasn't what made it art. You know?"

"I do know," Mead said suddenly, and I heard a deep breath as if he might go on. But that was all. After a second, I continued.

"So, is that what it means to really understand a work of art? That it belongs to you, deep down, it sinks into you so much that it feels like a piece of private property. Except—" I had slowed way down trying to get this right, but even so I was still puzzling it out. "—that even though it feels completely like *yours*, still at the same time it's not?"

Mead had closed his eyes again, but I could tell he was listening, "What I mean is that when I *knew*, absolutely *knew* what Morris was feeling and thinking, that wasn't spooky, that wasn't magic. That was more like realizing for the first time exactly *how* art sinks right deep down into you."

I found that I didn't really need Mead to agree with me. I just had to get it out there, like the rhyme word of a poem, like *fell* and *well*.

"Maybe not every time, maybe not everybody, but the thing that art lets you see is things that are inside you that are also inside somebody else. What you're thinking, what you're feeling in some part of you that is never going to see the light of day—somebody else must have had just the identical thought."

"And so that feeling," Mead said, suddenly sounding the way he had the first time he'd spoken to us, "that feeling makes you think you ought to keep the Tapestry for yourself?"

I laughed. "No, not at all, Mead! It's totally nuts: Now I'm completely positive it *should* go to a museum. That overwhelming feeling that it should just stay with me forever is exactly what proves it to me! I want everyone to want it the way I did. So I want the whole world to see it. I realize that makes no sense, but somehow my wanting never to let the Tapestry go is what lets me know that it's better off in the museum. So other people can feel what I did."

Mead stayed silent for a long moment. Then he nodded gravely and said, "Perhaps, young Jen, you should consider a new career."

"As an artist, you mean?" I said eagerly.

"Not at all," said Mead gravely. "In museum security!"

And to the sound of his chuckle I drifted off to a more peaceful sleep than I'd had in months.

It was hard to say how time passed at Kelmscott after that. Not quite sure what we were looking for, we stuck together as much as we could, me always toting my overstuffed gym bag, and Ed his bird-cage—even when he left it open the two remaining fledglings were perfectly happy to snuggle in there with open beaks pointed accus-ingly at us, waiting for bits of apple to drop in. I still had it in my head that we'd stumble on some perfect spring along the Thames, in a place well encircled by willows, and that Mead would be mended, just like that. But days turned into weeks, and our nightly explo-rations (who bothers to lock up a rowboat in rural Oxfordshire?) hadn't yet brought us to any spot that seemed likely to cure Mead.

One day, we were all securely tucked into the barn when we heard what could only be Morris trying to ride Mouse; a kind of *clip-clop clip-clop* punctuated by frequent grunts and the occasional "Tölt, drat you!" As the pair neared the barn, however, something odd happened. I knew we were securely hidden, yet somehow he'd chosen to pull up right beside us, Ed scribbling away, me nervously weaving and unweaving little wreaths of hay, and Mead dozing fitfully. I drew in a sharp breath and then tried not to move.

After a pause, Morris said meditatively, "Well, old Mouse, would you like it if I told you a story?" I half expected Mouse to respond, but all I caught was the faint sound of his big misshapen teeth chomping at a set of nettles that had grown up just under the edge of the barn floor.

Morris squatted down so that his back was actually leaning against the wall where we were sheltered. I was no more than the width of a barn slat away from him now. Close enough to hear his breathing and even, at one knothole six inches from my eye, to see a little bulge of brown fabric where the back of his woolen jacket was pushed against the wall.

"It's just a piece I've been working on for *Commonweal,* Mouse," Morris said at last, "a little parable about birds that I'd love to test out on a genuine bird, a strongly opinionated one." Morris paused, sighed deeply. "If I could only find the right bird.

"The Hammersmith League has asked me to speak about socialism," Morris went on after a pause, "and I had an idea that the best way to speak about the sorry sort of capitalism we all live under now would be to talk about England as if it were, well, what you might call an animal farm. In my story, the farmers stand for the bosses, of course, and the everyday workingman of England, well, he's represented by a common barnyard fowl. And most of the birds . . ."

He trailed off, as if he wanted to see who was listening. Though my heart was pounding, I tried not to give anything away, not a peep.

"Most of those birds—ducks, chickens, an awful lot of geese—they don't mind the farm." Morris was off again; you could hear his lecture-hall voice starting up. "Whatever those owners tell them to do, of course they'll do it—it's not as if they own themselves, after all. And so I begin the tale on a night they get together to debate among themselves the question the farmers have asked them, which is . . ."

He trailed off. And then spoke again, his voice seeming so sad and low I half expected a tear to roll through the barn wall. "Well yes, here, Mouse, I found myself stuck. What exactly are they debating?"

"With what sauce shall we be eaten?" The voice was so loud, so firm, that I almost jumped into the air. Mead, more awake than he'd looked in days, head cocked alertly, stared intently at the wall, waiting to see if Morris had heard him.

Morris roared with laughter. "With what sauce shall we be eaten?" he rumbled, "that's it! I see it perfectly. After hours of speeches"— now his voice grew louder and fainter, louder and fainter, as he wandered in circles nearer and farther from the barn wall—"yes, hours debating the merits of slow cookery and roasting, all those workers, I mean all those birds, argue themselves into an impasse.

"At which point," Morris said in a pleased voice, "an old and fat bird, with bedraggled feathers—"

"Or perhaps his feathers have all fallen out," I heard a voice say; mine! I clapped a hand over my mouth. Morris, without a glance toward the barn wall, went on quicker than ever, "Or perhaps all his feathers have fallen out, perhaps they have . . ." (Did he also whisper "O Girl of the Ledge"? I probably only imagined that.)

"In any case, he's nearing his end, but he still has some fight in him. So he takes a breath and he says . . ."

Again Morris trailed off, but this time the smile was in his voice and I knew that he had an answer waiting even if Mead had not at that moment rolled into a full standing position and said sharply, with all his old irritation, "In short, I don't want to be eaten at all!"

Morris's enormous laugh startled Mouse enough that he started trotting away from the barn. Morris followed him, muttering cheerfully, "Not eaten at all! Oh yes, that'll do nicely, that's the old bird spirit."

And looking at Mead, I understood with a shock it was quite true.

"Nobody's going to eat you, you old roc!" I said suddenly, fiercely ruffling what feathers he had left along his neckline.

CHAPTER FOURTEEN

Right Good Is Rest

After that, Ed and I redou-
bled our secret trips up-
and downriver, looking for the
willows that might mark the
spot Mead had mentioned.
Mead's steps, though, when he
left the barn at all, always drew us back closer to Kelmscott Manor
itself. "It's like he feels something growing inside it," Ed whispered
to me once.

We glimpsed Jane often now, at least once a day; I got the feeling
she made excuses to roam back near the barn to check on us. But she
never came too near; she was afraid, I guessed, of giving our hiding
place away—never even close enough for me to risk a wave.

Never, except that one evening just at sunset (Ed was down
sketching some kind of water bug in a river meadow) I came around

the edge of the barn suddenly and found her standing beside the sleeping Mead. She was holding what looked like a dead rat, pierced by a couple of long sticks. I sucked in a sharp breath and she turned around suddenly, dropping the rat at Mead's feet.

Instantly I was apologizing. "I'm so sorry, M . . ." and then I pulled up short, because I didn't even know what to call her. Oh, why wasn't Ed there?

After a long, appraising silence, the kind of pause that felt like we'd had a conversation, she held the rat up again for me to see. It was quite clear now: a skein of some beautiful soft gray thread, so thin and shimmery that in this light it almost looked like a bundle of spider silk.

"I'm so glad it's you, dear," she said softly. "Because you see I wanted to write a note to go along with this patching thread."

She lifted her hands helplessly. "Some people always know just what to say, don't they? May certainly does. But I expect I'd just have written something useless in the note, like . . ."

"What's undone can be done again," I said promptly.

Her eyes widened; after a second she gave little laugh. "Why, yes, that's certainly something that May would say. I must remember that one."

"But you're wrong," I said abruptly, and the hotness in my voice startled me. "You're wrong if you think that just because I'm a girl I know what to do with that thread. It's Ed you want if something needs mending . . ." I broke off suddenly, shocked how raw my voice sounded. What was I so mad about? She couldn't possibly know why I'd be embarrassed, even scared to see her again after throwing myself into her arms like that.

"No, dear," she said gently when it was clear I'd ground to a halt. "It's not for you; it's a gift. When I spoke with Ed, he told me a little about your grandmother and your . . ." Clearly at a loss for the right word. ". . . your voyage?" She shot a quick glance to see if I approved.

I took my closest, clearest look yet at Jane's perennially sad face. Here it was, the expression I'd tried to connect to the ill-fated marriage between Guinevere and Arthur or the love between Guinevere and Lancelot, or to Jenny's epilepsy. Maybe, though, I'd gotten it all wrong. Did some people just have sad faces, like freckles or a limp? Maybe that sadness was just part of who she was.

I looked down shyly and nodded yes. *Voyage,* a good word.

"Well," she went on, looking down at Mead, who stirred but didn't wake, "could you give your Granny this little present?" As she held it up again, I saw tucked into the thread not gray sticks but two beautiful little metal needles.

She had become more business-like and confident, speaking about the thread, holding it up slightly for me to see. "Of course it's not quite the same as sitting down at the loom; there is something, well, makeshift about the repair this thread will help your Granny do."

"Thread from Morris and Company," I burst out suddenly, light dawning on me. "With that kind of thread, nobody would ever guess—"

"Exactly!" said Jane with a delighted laugh. "It's just the same thread Morris and Company might use in the factory, if there were patches to be done before sending a piece off to its owner." Then she looked simultaneously pleased and guilty and glanced up at me—I must have had the same expression on my face, because suddenly we both laughed.

"I don't know much about your reasons for coming, Jen," Jane said after a long while, "but what I tell myself"—and something in her voice warned me not to correct her—"what I tell myself is that you're here because you care about what Topsy, and our May, and Ned and—" She hesitated. "—and all the rest of us have been doing."

I gave a vigorous nod, but she wasn't even looking at me now. Unconsciously she'd started stroking Mead's side, at a place where the glossy feathers still grew thick.

"I think I should thank you, Jen, because having a visitor from afar"—she held up a hand to make it clear to me she didn't want me to tell her anything more—"it's like feeling that you live on somewhere else."

I remembered a William Morris line that Granny had taught me, and without thinking I blurted it out. "Though I die and mankind liveth, therefore I end not."

To my surprise, Jane's eyes flashed indignantly. "Oh yes, that's very fine for Topsy to say, very fine!" she said bitterly. "But perhaps he could spare the occasional thought for those who live right around him. They're awfully hard to find when you need them, Mankind!"

My face felt as red as if she'd slapped it. After a minute, she swallowed and went on. "Yes, Jen, we live on in mankind, it's true, if we're artists and we make something just right, something that's not thrown away or left in an attic somewhere."

She paused, took a breath, and gently resumed stroking Mead's side. "But I don't think it's wrong to think of mankind a little less, and the people right around you a little more. Is it so bad to want people to know that you existed, that you . . ." Her voice thickened, and she stopped mid-sentence.

I wasn't sure I understood, but I made a sudden guess. "You want to know that the best things you did will survive you?" I asked. I found myself thinking of how we'd gone on without Mom and Dad for so long, trying to convince ourselves we were what was best in them, that we were carrying them forward with us.

"Yes," she said finally, "yes, I want what we did here to live on, even if it's only in part, or only in dreams. Even"—she gave a faint chuckle—"even bad dreams! What we did is worth an uneasy night or two, isn't it? Or so I tell myself sometimes in the dark, when I find I can't quite get to sleep." I wondered if I'd ever rid myself of that image of her, lying next to Morris (who snored, I was sure), trying to gather courage for the day to come.

Jane, though, suddenly smiled. Something about our conversation had cheered her. "And now, Jen, if you don't mind I'd just like to show you a few things about how I think this thread might be used. Could you watch me carefully?"

How long did we stay there? Days, weeks, months even. All I can say for sure is that one fall afternoon Ed and Mead and I found ourselves carefully circling into the front garden of Kelmscott Manor. I caught sight of *Commonweal* stuck up on the front door (OCTOBER 1896) as we did our best to stay hidden ourselves behind two drooping apple trees.

We were in luck: People sprawled lazily all over the tidy green lawns, and the talk rose from them in waves. Even the sound of two children and a horse-sized bird doing its best to pace stealthily across the gravel didn't reach them. Jane and Jenny sat upright in wooden chairs, bundled up tight despite the mild early-fall air—but they were smiling at something together. In fact, they were even starting to chuckle.

"Listen, Father," Jenny was saying in her frail, uncertain voice, "there was a lecture given in the city of Chicago, in America, by a Mr. Frank Lloyd Wright, called 'The Art and Craft of the Machine.' He says"—she switched into the worst American accent I'd ever heard, way worse than Ed's Sherlock Holmes voice—"'All artists love and honor William Morris, the great socialist.'" Morris gave a startled grunt.

"But the Art and Craft of the *machine?*" he exclaimed after a moment. "What does he mean by the machine?" Jenny and Jane giggled together in a pleased and friendly sort of way. "Oh let me finish, Papa," went on Jenny, squinting as she held her newspaper up in the bright sun.

"He says that you distrust the machine because in our time—I suppose he means in factories and armies—it is 'the deadliest engine of enslavement.'"

"Quite right," roared Morris immediately. "Why, I saw a factory floor in Leeds once that—"

May was lying next to Morris: she'd grown tall, nearly as tall as he, and her cheekbones had grown firm as her mother's, all her baby softness melted away. She chose this moment to drop a fat handful of apple leaves in his open mouth. He subsided, spluttering.

"Yes, Father," went on Jenny smoothly (she looked so happy in the sun today). "But you see, he also says that we have always had both handicrafts *and* machines, though we didn't like to admit how the two go together. See! Down here he even says that 'printing is a perfect representation of the Machine . . . human thought stripping off one form and donning another.'"

Morris had cleared his mouth now, but he wasn't barking an interruption. Instead, holding May's hand in his absently, he seemed to be thinking. "Yes," he said after a long pause, "yes, that's what I'd say, too. I think, Walker"—here he looked over his shoulder to Emery and Ned, both draped companionably over proofs from a medieval-looking book—"that's what I meant years ago when I said it was your photographs that allowed us to reach back to what was purest and best in medieval books. That's why John Ball and his peasantry belong in my *Nowhere*. Why should we not use what is here and in England, now, to save what is best worth saving from the past. Who needs complexity? After all, carving a potato to make a block print is terribly—"

"Simple," interrupted Jenny triumphantly. "That's just what this clever Mr. Wright says. Listen to what he writes: 'A work may have the delicacies of a rare orchid or the staunch fortitude of an oak, and still be simple.' He says that you, Father, showed that the best and 'highest form of simplicity is not simple like the side of a barn.'"

"Oh, dear!" said May, covering her ears automatically ("oh dear," said Mead, too, in the same voice, fluffing what was left of his feathers high and tucking his head low). A second later I realized why, as Morris gave an offended howl.

"So Mr. Wright is not impressed by the simplicity of the side of a barn," he shrieked in anguished, wounded tones. If his left leg had just been removed by a marauding tiger he couldn't have sounded more hurt. Yet with a flash of worry I couldn't help noticing that that he wasn't hopping around as he would have in earlier rages. *Like a grandfather clock,* I found myself thinking, *he's winding down.*

Still, Morris did find the energy to growl: "Have you ever *seen* the great Tithe Barn at Coxwell?"

"Actually, Father, yes," said May, "yes we have. You've taken us there a dozen times; once you even made Mother and Jenny go by bicycle, which frankly was . . ."

Morris was not even pretending to listen to May. He was stand-ing on a little patch of gravel as if he were on a podium in some Arts and Crafts society lecture hall. "Simplicity, elegance, fortitude, Oxfordshire's gift to world architecture has all these things. Mas-sive, low-slung, harmonious in all proportions, it has stood nigh on six hundred years, un—"

"Unapproachable in its dignity!" shouted Ned, Walker, Jenny, Janey, and May simultaneously. Morris looked around him vio-lently, opened his mouth to go on . . . and stopped, sheepishly.

"Well," he subsided, unwilling quite to let go of his point, "laugh at the simplicity of the Tithe Barn if you must. But I hope that Mr.

Lloyd Wright, and you May, and you Ned, find that you have made something with the massive simplicity you can feel in the Coxwell Tithe Barn. If you can feel that about a barn, or a chair, or"—looking over at the marked-up pages scattered in front of Ned and Emery— "a book, then I think you will have nothing to fear and little to regret when you come to the end of *your* life."

The stress he gave to the word *your* hit me—so did the way everyone looked down at the ground when he said it. I looked wildly around at Mead so he could tell me I was wrong. He, too, was looking at the ground. And Ed was staring at his William Morris notebook with a stony face; I'd never seen him so still. I started to reach over to check the first line of Ed's Morris book, the one where he had printed Morris's birth and death dates in neat letters. But something held my hands in place. Instead, I turned my head to listen to Morris one last time.

"I hope"—now Morris was almost back on his podium again, except that he had May's hand firmly in his, and was looking Ned in the eye—"you'll also feel you've made something that's beautiful and useful, something that reminds of how we might live, no matter how we do live now."

May picked up his hand again and planted a kiss on it; then another. "If any of us does make something that beautiful, Father," she said firmly (she kept her head bent low over the hand she'd just kissed), "you know very well it will be thanks to you. Who but you could have taught us" (and the way she said "us" I know she wasn't just talking about herself and Jenny) "to live *bigly* and *kindly*."

"Yes," broke in Burne-Jones, with some of the same confidence I remembered seeing in him the first time he'd spoken with the Pre-Raphaelites. "Whether the Arts and Crafts of the next century come from a pile of stones, or from a printing press, or from one of those machines that Wright and his Prairie School are building, you can be sure that they'll have a memory of you as firmly woven into them as, as, as . . ." Ned looked around, on the verge of tears.

"As that valence May is making for Mother and Father's bed," broke in Jenny unexpectedly—pointing.

May laughed—though the laugh had something heavy hidden deep inside it, like a stone in a blanket. She unfurled a bundle of cloth on her lap. "Yes, Father, have a look!"

Holding the long piece of soft wool in her lap, she put her head down and read, with only a slight tremble in her voice:

> *"No tale I tell*
> *Of ill or well,*
> *But this I say:*
> *Night treadeth on day,*
> *And for worst or best*
> *Right good is rest."*

As she finished reciting, I noticed with a start that her voice was growing fainter and fainter. I reached out to her, I even started to speak, but the wind had suddenly grown fierce. Ed, Mead, and I were caught up spinning up and away from Kelmscott Manor;

feathers would have made no difference in a gale like this. By the time I had grasped what was happening we were much too high to shout any final words. The only thing I could think of doing was to wave.

So I did, frantically, not caring who saw me now. I saw May, and Jane, even Ned and Emery and Jenny, standing suddenly with serious faces, standing and waving back at us. But Morris? He was lost in some thought, strolling away toward the Thames, head down and back turned. No amount of waving would reach him.

Then we were tumbling through the sky, with a storm cloud looming up behind us and the wind freshening. I pretended it was the gale that was making me tear up, and when Ed handed me his handkerchief he pretended to believe me.

"But, Mead," he was saying eagerly, maybe even angrily, "that can't be right, can it? How can we gather the Thames . . . ?" He was right. We'd certainly come to a place where the Thames ran chill, but what good did that do us, tumbling through the air with nothing to grab hold of, nothing we could bring back to finish off the Tapestry?

The wind roared and blew his words away. As we surrendered completely to its force, I remember thinking that I finally knew what Dorothy felt like. Only that was wrong: I wasn't heading to Oz, I was leaving it. And leaving too soon, leaving our job undone. Morris died young, I remembered suddenly; he died at sixty-three. Is this how he felt, too, pulled away when there was still so much to do? "What's undone can still be done," I found myself muttering over and over, "what's undone can still be done."

Although Ed had subsided into a grim silence, Mead was saying one phrase over and over as we tumbled together through the air. Before I could figure out what he might mean, we were passing over a little village churchyard where a funeral was going on. The church had on its harvest festival decorations, and the tombstone where the ceremony was going on was made of some simple gray stuff, tilted and smoothed till it looked like the hull of an old Viking ship. With a shiver, I recognized the three women who were drawn close around the grave—tight, tight, as if it were a feeble dying fire that they still somehow counted on for warmth.

Then everything sped up; it felt like something between a movie and a dream. First Oxford shot by—I caught a fleeting glimpse of those murals where Janey had once shouted, "Temper, temper." Then we were zooming down toward a little complex of factory buildings; the roof of one had its name picked out in thick white tiles: MERTON ABBEY FACTORY. And the next building: MORRIS AND CO.

As we tumbled down toward those buildings, I could finally hear what Mead was singing out over and over: "Not the *Thames*, the *mead*." It still made no sense to me. But I could tell right away it meant something to Ed. He clutched his birdcage closer, his face red and twisted with horror or dread.

Suddenly a downward gust left all three of us struggling to keep our balance. Then, as we tumbled downward, the wind without warning began to taper off. Within seconds it was down to a windy day on an inland lake; in less than a minute, nothing more than a gentle breeze.

Horrible as the wind had been, it had at least been our propul-
sion. Without it pushing us, where were we? Mead couldn't fly any
more than we could. He was a sad featherless lump a century from
home. Somehow managing to hold on to one another, the three of
us glided forward into the building marked Merton Abbey, not so
much flying as flung, coasting on the last of the gale that blew us
from Kelmscott Manor.

Inside, against the wall of a cavernous room, a redheaded old lady
sat at a loom alongside a teenager. Both spun around to stare at us,
wide-eyed—and I knew them both. But how? Hesitantly at first, the
teenager began to giggle softly with a hand over her mouth, as if she
didn't believe her eyes. The older woman, though, threw her head
back and laughed outright.

"Behold the roc!" she cried delightedly, "and the Girl of the
Ledge!" And she waved her arms over her head with a Morris-
like gesture there was no mistaking. "Yoicks!" I shouted at her
instinctively.

Although the wind had dropped inside the factory, Mead, Ed,
and I were somehow still moving forward, pulled now as much as
pushed. Somehow it came as no surprise to look up and see that the
wall we were heading toward had no window. Instead, hung along
its whole length was a beautiful old tapestry. No, I corrected myself
as Ed, Mead, and I barreled for it at full throttle, not a tapestry—
the Tapestry. Only this time, though the colors and the shape were

right, no picture was to be seen. Suddenly I had it: It hung with its back to us, where the knotted ends were. "We're coming out!" I yelled, and I thought I heard Ed grunt in delighted agreement. It's as if everything was happening in reverse.

As the distance closed and I braced myself for a crash, things started happening. There was a low booming sound, like faraway thunder, and I smelled what I now knew was Kelmscott's smell in a summer rain. At the same time, I felt the gym bag torn from my back—though I made a desperate grab for it, I felt it going, going. Ed's birdcage tumbled open, and I thought I saw one of the little fledglings struggle free into the air, wings moving furiously. And then, just before we struck the Tapestry again, Mead turned his head to me and slowly winked.

CHAPTER FIFTEEN

Down by the Willow

"**O**h! Oh! Oh!" I heard Granny saying. I opened my eyes to see her
staring down at me with an enormous smile.
"You've decided to rejoin us, I see!"

"Oh yes, Granny," I said, leaping up. "I
hope you didn't miss us too much while we
were gone." My head was still spinning, but
I wanted to clear things up with her right away. "I mean, of course
the police couldn't have tracked us in the nineteenth century—ha
ha!—so I guess you must have given up after a while and . . . Oh
Granny we have so many stories to tell you about what happened—"

I trailed off, because Granny—instead of giving me an *I am all
ears, my heroic adventurer granddaughter* gaze—was wringing out
a wet cloth she'd taken from my forehead, and just as efficiently
slapping another one down on it. A drop trickled into my ear. "Hey

Granny, stop! That's annoying!" I blurted out, sitting up, suddenly aware of a dull heavy throbbing in my right temple.

"Annoying it may be," she said crisply, pushing me back down so I rested against the wall, "but when young girls and *boys*"—she shifted her glare severely to Ed, whom I now saw slouched down beside me in the same undignified pose against the wall—"choose to go slamming their heads against very precious tapestries for no earthly reason, being nursed by their grandmother is *far* preferable to other things that might happen to them."

She paused, leaving us to take this in. Which Ed did before me. "But Granny," he said slowly, "there was a reason. We were chasing Mead . . ."

"Chasing a *mead*," Granny cut in sharply, with just a trace of her old English accent breaking through. "Do you mean a meadow?"

"No, Granny," I said, with a lurch in my stomach, "chasing your bird Mead! The one who belongs"—I was reassured to catch sight of it—"in that birdcage right over there." I pointed behind her.

She gazed at me as if I were a goblin or a changeling (and if you've never been gazed at by your grandmother as if you were a changeling, all I can say is that you're very lucky). "That birdcage," she said slowly, "was a gift from my old boss back in England. And it hasn't had a bird in it since . . ." She trailed off thoughtfully.

"Anyway, Granny," I said jumping up cheerily, "the good news is that we've found a way to save the house. I've just got to unpack this gym bag and we can figure out a way to . . ." I trailed off, because Ed was silently holding my tattered empty bag and his smashed birdcage up toward me. I was still digesting this when Granny said, in an astonished voice, "Whatever do you mean, save the house?"

"Why, from the bank!" I said immediately, whirling to face her.

Granny threw back her head and laughed, the kind of clear exuberant laugh I'd heard at Kelmscott Manor. There was no trace of worry in her eyes as she put her hand on my forehead. "Maybe that bump is deeper than I thought, Jen. It's not the bank that owns this house."

"But that letter . . ." I pointed up at the sofa, at what was clearly the terrible letter from Mr. Nazhar.

Granny handed me the letter with a smile. "It's just what we discussed, Jen. Mr. Nazhar proposes that the house will become the museum's Arts and Crafts Annex. All the things they've had from us over the years will come back here to stay, and we'll try to arrange them in the way their makers would have wanted. Like Emery Walker's house in London."

Despite the fact that my head was spinning—more from what Granny had said than from our flight down the Thames—I couldn't help asking, "Like Kelmscott House, you mean? With the blue willow wallpaper in the front hall, and the basement rooms with the Kelmscott printing press—"

"Or," interrupted Ed, "did you mean like Kelmscott Manor, with that long tree-lined walk, and those medieval tapestries with the gold lions that Morris liked so much better than anyone else did?"

As Granny gazed at us silently, bemusedly, I opened my mouth to apologize, to tell her that we were her good grandkids. Then I shut it again. I wasn't sure I was her good grandkid any longer, not in exactly the way she wanted me to be.

It didn't matter what I opened my mouth to say, though, because Ed, holding a notebook at arm's length above his head while flat on his back, was an unstoppable tornado of talk. "I think Webb would have wanted his glasses out on the painted sideboard," he was saying now, "and Burne-Jones meant for his drawings to be laid out on open tables. As for Jane's embroidery . . ."

I tried to kick him into silence, but I shouldn't have. Granny's face brightened as she sat before him, still wetting his forehead. "Do you think so, Edward?" she was saying, and "That's a remarkable thought about the woodblocks," and a moment later, "How on Earth did you come to think about the wallpaper that way?"—which she said in a tone full of love and admiration, every thought of alarm and surprise completely gone. The two of them looked at each other eyetoeye, one flat on the floor and the other kneeling above. The whole rest of the world could have stopped existing, leaving only Granny, Ed, and a museum filled with Arts and Crafts.

I was happy for them. But so many other thoughts were buzzing through my brain that I wasn't quite sure where my body even was. I did have a feeling there was one thing left to do. What was it, though, what was it?

I got to my knees and then to my feet, wandering vaguely round the room while trying to figure it out. I didn't want to leave Granny, did I? No, I was sure of that. I wasn't going to be her good girl anymore but not because I wanted to run away with Eva. I didn't have the slightest desire to play field hockey. In fact, from now on basketball in the backyard with Ed might suit me fine. That, and whatever sports they offered down at the high school for the arts, come next fall.

That would make Granny happy, but I wasn't doing it for Granny, nor for the reasons Granny had in mind. I loved the Tapestry, I knew that much, but I wanted it in the museum, and I could tell Granny why. Not because of the protective love Granny felt for everything that came down to her from May Morris. Granny would probably never understand what I meant when I said I didn't care anymore if Morris made the Tapestry, or any of it. But that didn't matter, either.

May was dead, and so was Morris. Saying that, even to myself, hurt, the way any wound does when you touch it. But it didn't make me change my mind. The Tapestry, and the Kelmscott books, and all the other beautiful art Morris had made didn't matter to me just because Morris made it. I cared about what was living in it, and what it meant to the living. "Let the dead bury their own dead!" I said fiercely—but Granny and Ed didn't even look up from their conversation about a piece of Burne-Jones stained glass.

Something else mattered, though, a lot. I still couldn't figure out exactly what it was. I went back over my thoughts, feeling hot and cold, my breath coming fast then slow. What was it? That I saw Morris die? No, it had something to do with how I had realized what made art alive. It was a conversation I'd been having with—

But Granny was speaking to us both now, tapping my shoulder for attention. Obediently, I followed her glance. "I can assure you," she was saying with a trace of a laugh in her voice, "nobody would doubt for an instant that this was a genuine William Morris tapes-try, perfect in every respect."

We turned to look, and for an instant I forgot to breathe. Those gaps we'd puzzled over for so long, the odd ellipses, lines and slender rectangles, were gone. In their place stood all the things we'd gath-ered. A pilgrim gourd and shell, a ship, a man with shield and spear, woodland beasts and a maiden in a red-gold crown. And the rest; all sewn into place (oh so smoothly!) with stitches so soft and fine that only someone standing way, way too close could have picked out the silver-gray thread that outlined a few perfectly normal-looking figures on a country landscape: an apple here, a dun rose there.

Granny, though, was still speaking. "Perhaps the notion of *authenticating* an artist's identity doesn't mean much to children your age . . ." She shot a sharp glance at us, daring us to tell her that we were too young to learn about artistic authentication. ". . . but if you look right down here"—pointing to our favorite meadow, where we'd first seen Morris on his fat little pony—"I fancy you can see where he's put down his initials. Yes"—she gave a little laugh—"there it is, do you see Edward, the telltale WM?"

I was focusing in on the spot she pointed to, but somehow I couldn't quite make sense of what I saw. What was wrong with me, why was I frozen like this? From a long, long way away, as if he were standing on a mountain, I heard Ed saying slowly, carefully, "Granny, I don't

think Morris signed his work, actually. He thought the work mattered more than the maker, and that in any case the making was almost always shared labor, and we've seen quite a lot . . ."

He trailed off. Then I heard his voice start up again, a little higher and faster, the way it sounded when he got nervous. "Um, Granny, where you see the WM . . . well, if maybe one of them was twisted wrong-way around to form the *M*, almost upside down, couldn't that little collection of lines be the claws of a bird? Not a WM at all."

And from even father away I could hear Granny answer, "Well, Ed, you may be right after all. Yes, it could be that what you see down there is one of Morris's favorite birds. It's the kind of little blackbird you'd see on the mead down by Kelmscott Manor."

I took a deep breath, tried to pretend that fourteen was old enough to be *mature,* to *face the situation bravely,* the way Granny told us to right after our parents died. I opened my eyes and looked down into my favorite corner of the tapestry, right where a knot of wil-lows grew along the Thames to form a kind of protected nook. Sure enough, looking back up at me from inside the tapestry, plain as day, every feather back in place, was Mead.

I don't remember how I got up to my room. But I do remember the next morning, when Ed woke me by tugging on my arm. Without bothering to tell him that I didn't want to, or I couldn't, or any one of the hundred other ways of telling him that I was not going to be mature about this, that I was not going to face the situation bravely, I just yanked my arm away and buried my head deeper in the pillow.

He shook his head and tugged my arm again. This time I gave up and let him pull me. Easier than fighting Ed when he got in one of these moods. I could sneak back up to bed later. As I followed him downstairs I was thinking gloomily how hard it was going to be to pretend I was overjoyed for Granny's new job. Her becoming the museum's residential Arts and Crafts curator seemed like a cruel joke right now. All it meant was that every day between now and when I went off to college, I'd have to see Mead's face looking out at me from the wall.

Still not meeting my eye, Ed tugged me into the living room. Setting myself with my back squarely to the tapestry, I faced him; Granny looked up from her knitting with a puzzled expression. I looked to Ed for an explanation. But all he did was stare intently at the birdcage. I moved toward it and froze. My hands went very tingly and my mouth was so dry I had to open and close it twice before I could speak.

Sitting inside the unlocked cage, calm and confident as if he'd been there all his life, was one of the birds Ed had grabbed with his hoodie in that willow tree near Nelson's Column. As we stared at him, he hopped to the edge of the cage, teetered there uncertainly for a moment, and launched himself into the air. I gave a yowl and leapt for the open window. But the bird, ignoring me entirely, circled our heads twice, zoomed by the Tapestry (did I just imagine that he brushed right up against Mead, down in his corner?), and landed on Ed's shoulder. As Ed and I jumped up and down whooping, he cocked his head at us quizzically, then opened his throat, tilted his head back, and gave a pathetic little cry.

I was almost through the kitchen door, where I knew I'd find an apple or banana, when a sudden idea struck me. "Granny!" She turned toward me, her usual expectant smile already sliding into place. "Granny!" I said again. Then, without rehearsal, without even a look at each other, Ed and I both tilted back our heads, waved imaginary swords, and shouted "Yoicks!"

Granny looked at us in stunned silence. Then, slowly, slowly I saw that same look of recognition that had spread across May's face at Merton Abbey Factory. Yesterday or seven decades ago. "Well," she said faintly, looking back at us as if she were trying to place us. Then her right arm shot straight up into the air, imaginary sword in hand. There we all stood, waving together.

The End

This book is typeset in Golden Type ITC Standard, a modern font closely based on the Golden Type that was designed by William Morris and Emery Walker for the Kelmscott Press and first used in *The Story of the Glittering Plain* (1891). Golden was inspired by the fonts of Nicholas Jenson (1420–1480), and in turn it inspired many better-known modern fonts that looked back to medieval typefaces for inspiration. Jenson trained in Mainz, Germany with "black letter" designers like Gutenberg; he then moved to Venice where he pioneered the elegant slender "roman" letters that are the basis for almost all modern typefaces. Golden Type is Morris and Walker's beautiful and distinctive compromise between the legibility of roman type and the dark bold forms of German black letter.

RAMSEY COUNTY LIBRARY
SHOREVIEW, MN 55126

J FIC PLOT
Plotz, John
Time and the tapestry : a
William Morris adventure /
SV   1086027
08/26/14

RAMSEY COUNTY LIBRARY
SHOREVIEW, MN 55126